CW00400384

Furry by Nature

Praise for 'Cornix Sinistra'

'A pan-dimensional tale, told with depth. Each of the chapters takes you further into a story that unfolds as you read it, with each alternate world as much a character in the book as the protagonists and heroine herself. A riddle wrapped in an enigma, it allows you to work out what is happening for yourself as the heroine struggles with the same issues as various protagonists seek to cheat, protect or recruit her. A satisfying read, which reminded me of a superior "Nine Princes in Amber" crossed with the classic "Sapphire and Steel".'
Amazon Reviewer.

Praise for 'Lore of the Sælvatici'

The easiest way I can describe the 'Lore of the Sælvatici' is to say imagine the 80s TV show Robin of Sherwood if it was stripped of its family-friendly tea time slot and was plunged entirely into the dark paganism that was only hinted at in the show.

It's bloody, sexual, atmospheric, and made up of 'discovered documents' hinting at a repressed folk movement from the dark ages, with the repetition of certain phrases suggesting an oral legend repeated to the faithful before, at some point, it was set down on the page before being lost - or hidden. And it leaves a hint that there may be more to come...
Jon Hartless, author of the 'Poppy Orpington' series

Furry by Nature

Steven C. Davis

Published by Tenebrous Texts

www.tenebrousarchives.weebly.com

First published in Great Britain in 2022
by Tenebrous Texts

Text © Steven C. Davis 2021 – 2022
Cover art © Nicky Rowe 2021 – 2022

All rights reserved. No part of this publication may be
reproduced, stored in a retrieval system or transmitted,
in any form or by any means, without the prior
permission of both the copyright holder and the
publisher in writing.

The right of Steven C. Davis to be identified as the author
of this work has been asserted in accordance with the
Copyright, Designs and Patents Act 1988.

This novel is a work of fiction. The names, characters and
incidents portrayed in it are the work of the author's
imagination. Any resemblance to actual persons, living or
dead, is entirely coincidental.

Typeset by Tenebrous Texts

www.tenebrousarchives.weebly.com

Dedication

To everyone who has helped bring the 'Less than Human' world into existence or supported it along the way. To Dave, Jerry, Nicky, to Anna, Ian and anyone I've accidentally missed. This is for you.

And to my friend, Sadism.

Part 1

Friday 1st April

'What am I going to wear?'

Rob sat up beside her. It was still early: only a pale glow slipped past the curtains. Her alarm clock blinked four thirty owlishly at her.

'Black is the tradition,' he caressed her long rumpled, crumpled, hair. 'It's still very early. The funeral isn't until this afternoon.'

'I know,' Nat reached out to stroke Rob's thigh. She could feel his strength, the warmth in his leg, the blood flowing in his veins.

'Do you want something to help you sleep for a while? I know they were a friend of yours.'

She shook her head. 'I'm not sure I want an aspirin or anything like that. You never know –'

'I wasn't thinking *that* kind of thing.'

Rob's hand eased across her ribs and onto her belly. She was aware of the feel of her own fur, heavy and thick, under Rob's hand. She wriggled closer to him and his other arm came round her shoulders, drawing her in, fingers stroking her chest.

Nat let her breathing slow. Rob. She closed her eyes. He was warm and smelled of the garden, or nature, as many Weres did, apparently, but also of dust. His scent was more undergrowth than tree or forest. If she could reach, she might have reached out for him. She didn't need to touch him to know he was hard, desiring her, even in her dishevelled state and on the morning of the funeral of a friend.

She'd been round to see them twice since Christmas. Had spent time with them; though they'd aged and could barely speak, their eyes had sparkled with life and they'd recognised her. She'd sat with them, their hand between hers, stroking the soft, wrinkled, skin.

'My Were Goddess,' Rob breathed.

Nat smiled, feeling her body tingle. When Rob spoke like that, more felt than said, his breath on her skin. She bit her lip. She wanted Rob, she did, she wanted him deep within her so she could scream her helplessness and tear his back.

'My furry Goddess.'

His hand on her belly stroked and caressed and tugged.

Nat rolled and turned, kneeling over him, kissing him. She put her hands on his shoulders, pressing her lips against his: he took her face in his hands, kissing her, opening his mouth to her tongue.

Nat tasted him, enjoying the feel of his hands on her cheeks, his tongue easing in to her mouth as she savoured him. Her chest tingled. She felt hot. Goose bumps burst across her skin and she shivered in delight.

Her knees wobbled and he wrapped an arm around her waist, pulling her onto him. He wrapped his other hand in her hair and pulled her head back, grinning for an instant before kissing her, devouring her, thrusting his tongue into her mouth and savouring her.

Nat clung to him, her back arched, kissing him passionately, wanting him desperately. She scrabbled at his back, wishing her claws would come through again, that she could use them to exhibit all the lust, the love she needed to, the desire, the helplessness.

He kissed her, licking her lips and laughing into her mouth.

'How do you want it?' Rob asked, eyes lust-fuelled.

'Hard and deep,' Nat answered automatically, blushing self-consciously simultaneously. She was almost bent backwards in his embrace, and it wasn't wholly uncomfortable, being held tight against him. 'I want to be underneath,' she elaborated.

He released her hair and cupped her bottom instead, lifting her away from him and turning with her, lowering her onto the bed.

'You don't need to,' her blush darkened in shade, 'eat me out. I'm quite – turned on.'

Rob grinned, stretching her legs out to either side of him. He ran his hands over her legs slowly.

Nat shivered. In the last few months she'd changed for Rob several times, and her body was adapting to it. She felt – younger. Fresher. Everything that had happened at SHiP – mattered, but not as much as it would have done six months ago.

Her legs were hairy. She'd never shaved her legs –
or anywhere – she'd never felt the need to, either with
Clovis or Gerald. Certainly not with Rob. But now red-grey
hair grew from ankle to thigh, not thick but fine. The
mound of rich red, soft grey fur between her legs was
thicker, deeper, spreading out towards both hips and
rising up her belly as if intending to engulf her navel. The
fur was a deep red immediately around and upon her sex,
but fading as it went outwards. Hair grew on her arms, soft
grey, but sparse for the moment.

He pulled her down so she lay flat on the bed, no
pillows. He put his hands firmly on her chest.

'My sister would tell you my type is busty women.'

Nat frowned. It wasn't exactly romantic pillow talk
to be talking about his sister – or other women – while he
was supposed to be paying attention to her.

'You've had other – Were women?'

He nodded, fetching a pillow and raising her up,
sliding it under her hips. 'I have. The majority of Were
women aren't busty. Whether it's something to do with
our creatures – women's creatures – wouldn't have boobs
so they don't –'

'Rob, there's better things you could be doing with
your mouth.'

He lowered himself down, kissing her, eating her
mouth, filling her mouth with his tongue. Nat clung to him,
her short nails almost scratching his back as she returned
the kiss.

He drew himself up after a few minutes, adding another pillow to the one beneath her hips.

'Now then,' he grinned.

--

Nat slipped her hand into Douglas'. He turned at the contact and smiled: Nat wrapped his hand in both of hers. The church was cold. The pews were hard. She felt – numb inside. She'd not been to a funeral since – since Kelly.

Kelly. Her step-mother. Adopted mother. The only mother she'd really known, since her biological mother – Nat gritted her teeth in concentration. She didn't want to think about that pathetic excuse for a human being; she was gone, as was her biological father, and no one cared about either of them.

But Kelly. She trembled slightly, and must have sighed, because Douglas gripped her hand tighter, looking at her compassionately.

She shook her head, managing to smile shyly. Douglas nodded and turned back to face the front of the church but his hand remained locked in hers.

Kelly. Kelly had known she was a Were. Kelly had loved her, and it hadn't mattered. If anything, Kelly had loved her even more because of it. Had brought her presents and treats when she had her period. Had continued to do so even after she came back from university, even if one of her presents had been introducing her to Gerald.

Gerald. Her ex. Lucie's partner. Lucie. Nat considered Lucie dispassionately. Rob's sister was interested in her, and Gerald didn't have a problem with that. Neither did Rob. She didn't know how she felt about that.

Having gone through to their bedroom for the puppy pile – months ago it felt like – Lucie and Rob had been in bed and waiting for them. Naked. They hadn't been touching or anything –

Nat wondered why they'd not tried having a puppy pile again. She loved Rob. She – she loved Robyn, but liked Lucie. Had no objection to Gerald. But the four of them –

To lie in bed surrounded by other Weres and a human who knew you were Were, whose lover was a Were, and who had brought up her brother, a Were. The idea of it – even without sex – was something she wanted to explore.

She had wanted to explore Lucie. To kiss her. To kiss her body, all the way down. To do things to – with – her while the boys watched. She had reached out, had gripped hold of Rob and Gerald –

She fought not to flinch in memory. There was a man at the front of the church saying something, but Nat was oblivious to him. There was only Douglas' hand in hers, and her memories of the puppy pile.

Lucie had changed. But she hadn't. Lucie wasn't a Were. She had seen a skull shining through Lucie's face. Had seen eyes of pure blackness where Lucie's eyes should have been. It had freaked her out so completely she had fled the room, fled the house – and been hit by a car.

Bruised ribs, a dislocated hip, a sprained wrist. Heavy scarring on the backs of her thighs and her buttocks from where she'd hit a brick wall. She'd got off lightly, though it was nothing in comparison to what her body went through when she changed.

Every bone broken. Muscles and sinews, veins, ripped and torn apart, shredded then reknitted in a new form. Incredibly painful, but she rarely remembered it. Going into a change from human to Were, it was like a full body orgasm or full body sneeze. Orgasm was a misnomer since it wasn't pleasurable, but an orgasm could trigger it. If she reached her peak and the orgasm didn't abate, if she continued building, peak upon peak, each orgasm higher and deeper than the previous, then it could trigger a change.

Going into a change from a Were to human, she thought it was tiredness. It took energy to maintain her Were form; to maintain a Were form. If she ate when she was Were, then maybe the Were would be present for longer, but the change always left her – left most who were Were – fairly wiped out for a couple of days. Rob was different; she guessed those he worked with might be similarly used to changing regularly and be able to regain their strength faster.

Nat didn't know why she'd seen the skull looming through Lucie's face. None of the others had seen it. But before that she'd seen her hand as a paw as well. It had felt like a change was coming, a really slow change, but it hadn't.

Am I losing my mind?

No. Rob – sensed something. He said it was like a change. But it didn't happen. It was after – she grimaced, holding still, aware the funeral service was still going on, aware of Douglas' grip on her hand anchoring her. After the examination from the doctor.

Maybe I reacted to something they'd given me.

She frowned. They didn't give me anything. Something on the gloves, or that ointment? Maybe just from, she grimaced again. It had been very unpleasant, having the doctor examine her internally.

She felt Douglas move and looked around. The coffin was being lifted up, to be carried out of the church.

Douglas' hand slipped from hers as they turned to follow the coffin with their gazes. They began filing out and Nat followed Douglas automatically.

She saw Clovis amongst the congregation, sat halfway down the church. She wondered why he hadn't been sitting with his father. A face she recognised, though it took her a moment – Councillor Barnet. Dr Gold, trying to look unobtrusive in a gold shirt and black jacket.

The afternoon sunlight was a surprise, though it shouldn't have been. It was April and the sun was bright, causing her to shield her eyes for a moment.

'We're having the wake at my house, Nat,' Douglas said, drawing her into his embrace and kissing her head.

She hugged him back, surprised for a moment that he held the hug for so long.

'If you'd like to join me in the lead car, Nat, we're heading back to the house now.'

'Aren't we – normally the – graveyard?'

Lord Merryweather shook his head. 'That was not their request. I will explain later, Nat.'

She noticed Clovis appeared to be talking to a woman with straw-gold hair in a dark business suit. The woman seemed to be smiling.

'Who is that,' she asked, 'with Clovis?'

Douglas glanced and smiled. 'That is Felicita. Clovis' escort. We'll talk about her later.'

Nat nodded. 'The one that you –'

Douglas nodded.

--

Douglas opened the door for her and offered his hand. She took it and stepped carefully out of the car. Smoothed her skirt and blouse down. Stockings – because – and a suspender belt. Flat shoes. She wasn't wearing so little beneath her clothing to be – flirty. Or because Rob had ordered her to. It was a warm day and a slip would only make her perspire. Knickers – even tights – were unable to contain the sprawling thicket between her thighs.

'It seems so long ago that you first came here.'

Nat blushed. 'The ball. Where I met Rob,' her blush deepened.

Douglas nodded, smiling mildly. 'Yes. You were the guest of honour, Natalayiana. Everyone wanted to dance with you.'

She took his proffered arm. 'And you let me think you were the chauffeur, or something similar.'

Douglas chuckled. 'I did.' He sighed, gently. 'And then you met Clovis,' he nodded to the man holding open the front door of his house. 'And for a while, realising *you* were the one my son had had − relations with − at university, I thought my first impressions might be wrong.'

'And what were your first impressions, Douglas?'

He grinned, taking her through to the main hall. Tables had been set up with food and drink. Waiters milled about; three moved in to intercept them, each carrying glasses of wine and hors oeuvres.

'Even − just before Christmas − you would not have been so comfortable calling me Douglas.'

Nat blushed. 'You don't −'

He chuckled. 'Nat − relax.' He smiled. 'My impressions were that there was little you wouldn't do or try to help someone. Now, why don't you come round Sunday afternoon and we'll have a proper talk about things.'

Nat nodded. 'I'd like that. This thing with Clovis −'

Douglas nodded, glancing beyond her for a moment. 'Now then. Laetitia is circling, but Clovis and Felicita are by the drinks. I suggest you go and introduce yourself to Felicita; I'll divert Laetitia.'

Nat smiled. 'Thank you. I'll see you Sunday.'

Douglas took her hand and kissed it. 'Sunday,' he grinned, wheeling away.

Nat hurried over to Clovis.

'Clovis. Won't you introduce me to your friend?'

Clovis and the woman turned. 'N – Natty. Nat, I mean.' Clovis blundered awkwardly. 'This is Felicita. Pa suggested she accompany me, so I get used to having a woman on my arm at social occasions.'

Nat raised an eyebrow. 'It's a funeral, not a date.'

'We're not dating,' Felicita interjected. 'Lord Merryweather has paid for me for the rest of the day, so it's my choice if I stay for an hour or so and go, or let Clovis take me upstairs and entertain me.'

Closer up, her hair was more blonde-gold than straw-gold. A plain face, Nat would have said, but well made up. A trousered business suit but beneath the jacket Felicita was wearing a red lace top that left a reasonable amount of bosom bared. Clovis was openly staring down her top.

'Clovis,' Nat spoke softly, 'you shouldn't be staring down your date's top.'

Felicita laughed, earning a few looks from those nearby. 'I do not mind. I have desirable natural assets.'

'You do,' Nat nodded, 'and of course you should show them off, but Clovis –'

'But she's displaying,' Clovis protested, waving his hand at Felicita's chest.

Nat raised her eyebrows, looking at Clovis.

'Clovis, it's not really polite to stare at your date's chest and not her face. It's not –'

'It is not a date,' Felicita repeated, scowling. 'Lord Merryweather bought me for the day to accompany his son. It is my choice if look is all he can do or if I will let him play with them later.' She looked at Nat coldly. 'I find it is so easy to distract men when you have a shapely bosom for them to play with.'

Nat scowled.

Felicita laughed, putting her arm on Clovis' arm. 'Come, Clove. Show me the grounds of what will be your property one day.'

'Er, one day,' Clovis blushed. 'Pa's not – I mean, he's old, but not that old. It might not be for several years, rather.'

As they walked away, Felicita pulling Clovis along, Nat felt a presence next to her.

'Well, that went well.'

She turned, slowly, forcing herself to remain passive.

'Dr Gold.'

'Dr Gold?' Laetitia drawled. 'After you rang my bell so eagerly, Natalayiana? After you knelt on a station concourse to eat me out so thoroughly.'

Nat blushed. 'What – what are you doing here?' she demanded.

Dr Gold smiled. 'Vic was a patient for a long time. I wouldn't call him a friend, but I spent a long time with him. I will miss him.'

Nat nodded, unsure what to say, wanting Douglas or someone – anyone – to rescue her.

'And you, Natalayiana? How is it having your good looking friend sleeping on your sofa a couple of nights a week?'

'Robyn is doing well for it, knowing she's safe from – you.'

Laetitia smiled sweetly. 'The mummy of a girl whose father is a Were. Has Rob fucked her yet?'

Nat blushed. Shook her head. 'No. Of course not.'

She chuckled. 'Really? His type is busty. You are not his type. I was expecting him to plough you and move on, leaving you free for me to take.'

Nat blushed, aware those near her were scandalised and pretending to speak, listening, waiting to hear what else the doctor would say.

'Rob and I are –'

'You like being fucked by a Were?' Laetitia spoke softly, her eyes narrowed. 'Knowing he could change inside you at any moment?'

Nat shook her head desperately. 'It's not like that. He has good control. How did you know –'

Laetitia snorted. 'Everyone knows who Rob works for. He's fast. He's strong. He's big. I can even tell you what his Were is, if you don't believe me.'

Nat shook her head desperately. 'It's not –'

'Miss Harewood?'

Nat looked up, and smiled in relief at Councillor Barnet. 'Councillor?' She offered him her hand and he seized it, shook it enthusiastically.

'Oh, do please excuse me, Doctor Gold. Natalayiana, I wanted to thank you for going round to visit Vic so often in the last few months. He was very taken with you.'

Nat blushed awkwardly, noticing the doctor peel off, still watching her. 'I liked going to see him. I still can't,' she shook her head. 'I knew he was – declining – but he thought he had another summer left in him.'

The councillor nodded. 'I think that was what he told people. He didn't like people making a fuss of him. Very understated, he was. Shy, almost.'

'You – knew him long?'

Mr Barnet nodded. 'Indeed.' He smiled, a little too brightly. 'I hope at some point soon, we get to meet and play cards again. In Vic's memory.'

Nat nodded. 'I would like that.'

--

'Rob?' Nat called out, locking the door behind her.

Rob appeared, a tea towel in his hands. He grinned, dropping it on the back of the sofa. 'How are you feeling?'

Nat stood on tiptoe to kiss him. 'Like I want to be reminded I'm alive.'

Rob grinned, unbuttoning her blouse. 'You know what they say is the best thing for that.'

Nat stopped him before he completely unbuttoned it but he slid his hands inside, fingers on her torso, thumbs pressed against her nipples.

'Sex is your answer to everything,' she smiled.

Rob shrugged, rubbing his thumbs in opposite directions. 'There's not much it doesn't make better.' He grinned. 'But maybe to round the evening off later tonight.'

Nat raised an eyebrow. 'What had you in mind?'

'The sun will still be up for several hours. I would like to see you sunbathing nude in the garden.'

Nat stared. 'The neighbours will see!'

He shrugged, disentangling his hands and drawing her closer against him.

She could feel his interest, hard against her belly.

'What will they see?'

'I'll be naked.'

He shook his head. 'They're an old couple across the way. Your sex is covered by your fur. You're flat chested. They'll think you a boy.'

Nat snorted. 'I'd still be naked. And I know you, Rob. You'd want to fuck me outside. They'd think you're fucking a young boy.'

He grinned, stroking her back. 'That's true. If I found somewhere private, would you consent to sunbathing nude and making love outdoors?'

Nat put her hands around him, stroking him through his trousers. 'I could – have a go at that. Some of that, definitely.'

Rob grinned. 'And if I put a couple of golf umbrellas up outside?'

Nat tilted her head. 'Then we wouldn't be sunbathing.'

Rob dropped his hands to caress her rump. 'How about a compromise?'

'What had you in mind?'

'One deckchair. I'll go out in shorts. You can join me later as you are.' He smirked. 'Of course, I would expect you to draw your skirt up all the way before you sat down. And, maybe,' he hesitated.

Nat raised an eyebrow.

'Once you were sat in my lap, you could lose the blouse.'

Nat gave him a look. 'You just want me naked, outside.'

Rob nodded. 'Yes. I find you beautiful, Nat. You are a Were goddess. I want you on my arm to show off and I do mean naked.'

Nat blushed. 'I couldn't – the thought of being topless is – challenging. I can build up to that. But not – full. Not in public.'

Rob cupped and squeezed her cheeks, kneading her bottom. 'How about we start somewhere – less scary for you?'

Nat leant against him, enjoying the feel of his intent, hard against her belly and the feel of his hands.

'What did you have in mind?'

'One deckchair,' he grinned. 'You sit on my lap. We kiss, we cuddle. After a while, when you're ready, I'll put a hand up your skirt.'

She kissed his cheek. 'I should go and change out of the black.'

He gripped her tighter. 'I like you in black. But you might want to lose your knickers.'

Nat rubbed herself against him. 'I'm not wearing any.'

Rob raised an eyebrow, squeezing her cheeks even tighter. 'You mean you went to a funeral without any knickers on?'

Nat nodded. 'But I am wearing stockings and a suspender belt.'

He stopped gripping her so hard and began feeling her up until he found the suspender belt and pinged it.

'Bad girl,' he grinned.

Nat nodded. 'When we move inside,' she stood on tiptoe, wriggling until she could kiss him on the lips, 'when you take me inside later, take me up to the bedroom and put me across your lap. Draw my dress up and –'

'I'm tempted to do that now,' he grinned.

Nat shook her head. 'You wanted me naked outside. I'm not comfortable, I can't. But I can sit in your lap and after a while you can finger me. Make me come, outside.'

Rob grinned, kissing her, kissing her passionately until she had to pull away to breathe.

'I don't normally drink, but I'd like a glass of wine. You?'

Rob nodded. 'I'll join you.' He pulled her round and finished unbuttoning her blouse. 'I'm not saying take it off,' he moved to stop her protest. 'Just – a little riskiness. You'll be sat on my lap, anyway.'

Nat nodded, slowly. 'Okay.' She smiled. 'I'll get the wine.'

'I'll get the deckchair.' Rob grinned.

Nat poured them a glass each of wine. That last time at Vic's. If I'd known. She sighed, softly. Remembered just sitting with him, holding his hand. Helping him to a sip of water – he'd been unable to manage anything solid, and didn't want tea.

Rob swatted her bottom in passing. 'Come on, you. Don't get maudlin.'

She followed Rob out into the garden. The walls to their neighbours' sides were reasonably high enough; anyone in those gardens couldn't look into theirs, unless they were at an upstairs window. But the garden backed on to the end of another garden, and the wall wasn't that high, that opposite garden well maintained and near pristine.

Rob put the deckchair down and opened it out, settling down, unbuttoning and unzipping his trousers a little.

'Hey, I want you to be able to reach things – if you want to reach things.'

Nat smiled, putting the glasses down on the ground slightly behind the deckchair. She settled down into Rob's lap, leaning in to kiss him properly. He was warm and eager – she could feel him, hard against her thigh.

'Lose the shirt,' she ordered.

'Now who's giving orders?' he grinned, making no move to unbutton it.

'Lose it or I'll spill wine down it,' she stretched past him, picking up one of the glasses. 'And that would be a waste.'

He grinned, unbuttoning it, sitting up, forcing her to sit carefully as he peeled it off and discarded it.

'Better.' Nat grinned. 'Whoops.' She splashed wine across Rob's chest. She put the wine glass down and leant in, licking it up, enjoying the feel of his skin against her tongue. His belly tightened and she nibbled a little, licking at the damp, tight muscles.

Nat sat up, grinning. 'Who knows where I might spill my wine, later.'

Rob grinned, pulling her in for a kiss, one hand sliding inside her shirt. She thrust her tongue into his mouth, grabbing his chest and groping him.

After a while they broke apart, Nat licking her lips. Rob was breathing heavier; she knew she was flushed as well.

'I might not have tits, but neither have you.'

Rob grinned, fetching his wine glass. He took a mouthful of wine and held it, pushing the blouse from her shoulders singlehandedly. Still holding the mouthful of wine – and grinning wickedly – he rolled the glass over her stiffening nipples. He leant in, sucking one, teasing it with his tongue.

As he shifted from one to the other Nat moaned, grabbing his hair.

He bit and she yelped, feeling him lick, feeling the wine in his mouth. He lifted his head and kissed her, breathing wine into her mouth and making her hiccup in surprise.

Rob chuckled, pulling the blouse from her back and discarding it.

Nat stared in surprise, hiccupping. Automatically she clapped hands to her chest but the world didn't end, the neighbours didn't scream abuse or wolf whistle.

'You see?' Rob smiled. He took her hands away from her chest gently. 'Nobody can see, and nobody cares, apart from you and I.'

Nat blushed. Rob sat up, folding her into his embrace, kissing her soundly. Nat ran her fingers down his back, enjoying his shudders.

Rob broke the kiss, kissing her nose. 'The world has not ended. Seriously, Nat,' and he smiled, his eyes gleaming with lust, 'I hope the time comes when I can tie you naked to a tree in a forest and cane your backside.'

Nat looked up at Rob, terrified by the idea, and a little bit turned on. 'Not in a – public park.'

He kissed her again, and drew her back against him, arms wrapped around her. 'Maybe not a public park. But somewhere deep in a forest, miles from anywhere.'

Nat shivered. It was a fantastic, outrageous, scary idea – and yet –

'Somewhere miles from nowhere. Somewhere I can undress you, unhurried, and kiss every inch of your body. Somewhere I can tie you up, and cane your bottom. And having done that,' he grinned, 'I'd take you from behind.'

Nat shivered again, turned on and cautious. She kissed him on the cheek. 'Do you want my Were running wild?'

'Then or now?'

She smiled, resting her head on his chest. 'You've only spanked me with your bare hand before.' She stroked his chest. 'Would you like to use a cane, or other things on me?'

He nodded. 'If you enjoy it, I want to try it.'

Nat blushed. 'I haven't – actually – been caned before. Even when I was a girl. But I would like to be – not a good girl.'

Rob chuckled. 'You're a born naughty girl, Nat. If I told you to wear knickers to work next week?'

Nat snorted. 'I wouldn't. But only so I'd get in trouble.' She smiled awkwardly. 'Although there are – reasons.'

'Reasons?'

'Reasons.' She kissed his neck. 'This might work – better – if I was sat side on to you.'

'You would be more – open. Exposed.'

Nat disentangled herself and stood up. For some reason, standing up and being topless was scarier than being sat astride someone and topless. She looked up at the neighbours' houses, wondering for a moment if there was anyone in the bedrooms, watching her.

She watched Rob as he shifted position, unzipping his trousers and pushing them further down.

'So you have – access.' He grinned.

Nat drew her skirt up to her thighs: up just high enough to show the stocking tops and the suspender straps. Rob growled lustfully.

She sat in his lap demurely, sliding her hand inside his trousers. He was hard, trapped by his pants and trousers. She stretched her hand along his length.

'I'm not – comfortable – with giving you a blow job outside.'

Rob's gaze narrowed slightly. 'You're not okay with blow jobs in general, Nat, and I'm okay with that. I'm not going to force you – or ask you – to do something you're not comfortable doing.'

'But you always,' she blushed. Rob knelt before her often, or laid her on the bed or the sofa or elsewhere, and tucked his head into her lap.

He laid his hand on her thigh, stroking her leg softly. 'I don't eat you out, Nat, so you'll give me a blow job in return. I bury my face in your fur and use my tongue on you because I like being that intimate with you when you climax. I like tasting the pleasure on your lips.' He eased his hand higher up her thigh. 'It turns me on to eat you, Nat.'

Nat blushed. Felt his fingers touch her fur. Felt a frisson of excitement run through her. His other hand was on her back, stroking and tracing patterns on her skin. She ran her hand down his chest. Down his belly. Lower.

'You're going to bring me. Outside.'

'Yes.'

Rob smiled. His fingers curled in her fur, tweaking and tugging.

Nat shifted position slightly, giving him better access. She bit her lip as his fingers inched beyond the top of her stockings, as they brushed over her inner thigh. In the midst of her undergrowth he found her lips and stroked them softly.

Rob leant in, licking and kissing her nipple. 'Is it wrong,' he whispered to her chest, 'that I want to pull you up, pull your skirt up, that I want to put you on my face and eat you here and now?'

Nat stroked his cheek softly. 'No, it's not wrong. It's not going to happen, either.' She smiled softly. 'I find,' she kissed him again. 'I find I don't want to be fingered. Even outside.'

'Oh –'

She nestled in against him. 'What I do want, is for you to tell me what you would do to me – if I let you.

Suppose we were in the middle of nowhere. No neighbours.'

Rob wrapped his arms around and drew her in closer. She tucked her knees in to his chest: he eased her skirt up until his hand was resting on her hip.

'What would I do with you?' he grinned. 'I think there would have to be the potential for a little bit of humiliation. Some of what Dr Gold did turned you on.'

Nat blushed. Nodded.

Rob caressed her hip. 'I have a suggestion. Robyn has said –'

'Several times,' Nat interjected.

He nodded. 'I love you, Nat. I will take you upstairs shortly, tie you up, spank you and make love to you.'

Nat chirruped in delight, nibbling at his throat.

'You know Robyn's offer.'

Nat nodded.

'I am not doing this because it is Robyn, Nat. I am happy with her coming round two or three nights of the week, it gives her and Mildred stability, it puts the doctor's nose out of joint.'

Nat grinned.

'But I would like to take her up on her offer. If you are okay with it.'

Nat sat up, kissing Rob, teasing him until he opened his mouth to her; she thrust her tongue in, exploring, barely aware of his hands on her back, on her rump.

'I'm okay with it.' She smiled, realising Rob's hands were on her rump, that her skirt had been pulled up over her hips. 'Why wouldn't I be?' she grinned. 'To make love to the man I love and the woman I love.' She ran her hands along his shoulders. 'I will check with Robyn. I think she will be okay with full penetration.' She sniggered. 'I want to watch the pair of you fuck. I want you to watch Robyn and I fuck.'

Rob grinned, removing one hand from her arse and sliding it between her legs; cupping and squeezing her tenderly. 'You know it will only be a one-off. We don't need anyone else in this relationship, there's already four of us.'

'I know,' Nat nodded, trying not to feel disappointed.

Rob cupped and stroked her gently. 'You said you would be up for a little bit of humiliation?'

'Yes,' Nat answered, feeling hot and wary at the same time. 'Robyn wouldn't be –'

Rob shook his head. 'I wasn't thinking humiliation with Robyn. Robyn – doesn't know our secret.'

Nat nodded. 'I will – tell her. Just not yet. After,' she promised.

Rob grinned. 'Okay. But I was thinking.'

Lust bloomed in his eyes. His fingers were stroking her, his middle finger almost parting her lips. She was half naked in the back garden – realised his other arm was around her waist, holding her. Bare bottomed in the back garden. It was – a little bit – but not enough to make her run. The sun was warm on her bare skin, and it was lovely.

'What were you thinking?' she asked, her hands on his chest.

'I'm thinking a holiday cottage,' he grinned. 'Us,' he tilted his head, thinking about it, 'Gerald and Lucie as well. A Were weekend away.'

Nat shifted as Rob eased his finger between her lips.

'You're not dry,' he murmured. His other hand slid down from her waist, between her cheeks.

Nat blushed. 'You were thinking a – Were orgy?'

'Kind of.' Rob leered. 'At some point you will be tied up and blindfolded so you don't know who's doing what to you.'

Nat leaned in and kissed him. 'We will talk about this some more, but in general, yes. Now.' She leered at Rob. 'There should be a finger in my front and another in my bottom.'

--

Nat smiled, stretching her arms out in readiness. Rob had already bound her ankles to the corners of the bed. She was nicely spread, bent over the end of the bed. Rob had taken the skirt off her, leaving her in stockings and a suspender belt.

'That is a lovely view.' Rob paused behind her, kissing her cheeks. 'Some light discipline first,' he moved up beside her, taking her wrist, knotting the rope around it.

'It doesn't have to be *that* light,' Nat murmured.

He grinned, tightening the rope around her wrist. 'I've found a nice steel ruler. That might sting quite a bit.'

He bound her wrist to the headboard.

'Are you really okay,' he asked, sitting beside her, stroking her back, 'with having a threesome with your best friend?'

Nat turned her head; kissed his knee. 'I am. I want to experiment more. I'm okay,' she blushed, 'with the thought of being tied up and blindfolded. Of having you, Gerald and Lucie there.'

He leant in and kissed her softly. Walked round the bed, slapping her rump in passing, She quivered. He looped the other rope round her wrist and pulled it tight.

'And you're okay – with Gerald being there? With him – potentially – doing things to me?'

He bound her wrist to the headboard. Was silent for a long moment. 'You did things with Dr Gold. I would far rather have been there, even if I could only watch.' He grinned, caressing and squeezing her cheeks. 'You are beautifully spread and available, Nat.' He slipped his hand between her cheeks.

Nat shivered. It hadn't been wholly comfortable – or uncomfortable – when Rob had used his fingers on her earlier.

'I want to watch your ex – and my sister – having their wicked ways with you.' He pulled his hand back and slapped her. 'I want you to be as confident as you can be. And to have as much fun as we can.'

Nat shivered. The ropes binding her were tight, tight enough to pull her out and stretch her into a starfish position. What Rob had down – downstairs – had turned her on. Not enough to orgasm, but she knew she was close.

'And you? What's fun for you?'

Rob chuckled. 'My girlfriend wearing nothing but stockings and a suspender belt, tied face down over our bed. Her plump little arse is going to get a good drubbing.' He bent in and kissed her cheeks. 'And when I'm ready,' he stretched out over her.

She could feel him, hard, against her cheeks. He slipped his hands under her chest, groping her.

'When I'm ready,' he repeated, nibbling at her neck, 'I'm going to take her as hard as I can, in her hot, wet, tight, little pussy.'

Nat deliberately wriggled, tugging at the ropes. Rob pulled back.

A moment later, his palm struck her cheek. She wriggled as provocatively as she could and he struck her three times in quick succession. Nat bared her teeth, a spasm causing her fingers and toes to twitch.

She heard the sound before she felt the pain: howled, her body whiplashing. She was aware of her cheeks burning, the stinging that was quite strong.

'Was that – too much?'

Nat rubbed her hips. The warmth in her bottom, particularly from that strike, was quite pleasing. 'You need to gag me if you're going to use that. It stings quite a bit.

It is painful,' she turned to look at Rob. 'Gag me. Keep using it. I will orgasm. While I am still shuddering, you need to get inside me and take me as hard as you can.'

'Are you sure?'

Nat smiled. 'We buried Vic today, Rob. We are Were. I want to feel another Were inside me – in human form. I need to be loved. I need to be fucked. I need to climax from what you do to me. I need to be,' she smiled; grinned. I need to be out of my head. Out of my body.

Rob fetched one of his shirts. She opened her mouth obligingly and Rob eased most of it into her mouth, knotting the arms tightly behind her head.

'Better?'

Nat nodded, gesturing with her head at the ruler.

Rob picked it up. Struck her with it.

Nat howled, screaming into the shirt.

Rob nodded. 'Barely anything. The neighbours won't hear your cries.' He stroked her back. 'You are going to have a very tender and sore bottom. It may be uncomfortable to sit down for a few days.'

He struck her and Nat cried out. He struck her again, in exactly the same spot, and Nat howled, whiplashing against the restraints. A third, a fourth, a fifth, time.

Nat squirmed. Tears were running down her cheeks. Her bottom felt like it was on fire. She could feel the orgasm building, the warmth in her belly, her nipples like little rockets. Her legs trembled. Her arms quivered.

Pain flared again and again and again and again across her bottom. She felt like she was adrift. There was nothing but the burning, coruscating, pain in her cheeks. The afterglow, after the initial spike of pain, was delicious, but the afterglows were being buried in the coruscations and she screamed, lifting her shoulders, putting her weight on her hips, tugging at the ropes –

The metal ruler bit into the same stripe of tender skin and Nat howled, arching her back, tearing the ropes loose –

She was there and in heat, in season, clawing at the soft/hard and her mate was there, pulling at her. She jumped onto the soft/hard, lashing him with her tail. He followed, pinning her, trying to pin her. She tried to lash again but he was too close, biting at her ears, his paws grabbing her fur. He pushed into her and she pushed him away, wiggling her hips. He needed to be bigger, better, more active –

She jumped onto the ground, chittering. She was in season and wanted him, needed him, but he had to be better than her – he jumped on her, his paws on hers, pinning her tail to her back, and then he was over her, inside of her, taking her –

Sunday 3rd April

'I need to see Lord Merryweather.'

Nat sat up and looked around. She was lying on a new mattress in their bedroom. The windows were ajar and a warm, summery breeze drifted in.

'Rob?'

He walked in, carrying a tray with a plate of food and a steaming cup of tea on it. 'You changed,' he smiled.

'The mattress?'

His smile flicked to a grin. 'Your Were shredded it. You could have said something.'

Nat shook her head. 'I didn't –' she sat up slowly. 'What time is it?'

'Early afternoon. Sunday.'

Nat nodded, reaching for the tea. 'Thank you.' She clutched it, two handed. 'I hope you didn't have plans for yesterday.'

Rob smiled, shaking his head. 'You needed – to feel alive – after the funeral.'

Nat took a sip of the tea.

'What does Lord Merryweather want to see you about?'

She shifted, trying to feel if there were any aches or pains, any bruises, on her bottom.

'Your bottom was flushed quite pink before you changed. Afterwards, not so much.'

Nat blushed. 'I needed to change. You didn't – mind?'

Rob grinned, leaning in and kissing her. 'Why would I mind? My lover's an animal.'

Nat's blush deepened. 'I was – it was good.' She reached out and stroked his arm. 'I liked being tied up and tanned. Maybe not so hard or so fast next time, if you don't want me to change again.'

Rob grinned, sitting on the bed next to her, kissing her. 'Or we do, but we have Lucie with us.'

Nat frowned. 'I know – Gerald has said, he can go a lot – further – with her and know he's not going to shift.'

Rob nodded. 'I would like to know more, but I don't know how to do it without risking Lucie. My people – if they knew that some people could –'

'Take energy?' Nat suggested.

Rob hesitated. Nodded. 'Yes. I think that's it. There were times – when I was younger. I wasn't always good at – not changing. But Lucie helped me; just being near me.'

Nat nodded slowly. Formless thoughts were churning in her mind.

'Your – the people you work for,' she said, finally. 'They're – official?'

Rob nodded. 'An unofficial official government department.'

Nat shook her head. 'No. We Were,' she paused. 'There's you and Gerald. Lucie, who's Were-friendly. Jack. He's,' she hesitated. 'He's Were, but he works for Homes for Weres.'

'What are you thinking?'

Nat shook her head. 'Something that couldn't possibly be.'

'What?'

Nat shook her head again. 'No. I need to think about it. I need to go and see Lord Merryweather, as well.'

Rob nodded. 'When you're ready, I'll take you.'

--

'Nat,' Lord Merryweather beamed, stepping back. 'Please come in.'

Nat entered. Lord – *Douglas* – embraced her quickly. 'You are well?'

Nat nodded. 'I woke up late this morning. Friday seems – so long ago.'

Douglas took her arm and escorted her into his study. The art on the walls was all 1920s pinups, innocent and powerful at the same time. Images of women – barely clad – but clothed enough that nothing showed or showed through. Mostly black and white, some re-colourised, but uniformly beautiful and powerful. All were incredibly erotic and in most of them the models were not trying for erotic but reading a book or reclining on a bed, attempting to sleep. So much more powerful than the porn she'd had growing up; the porn she still used now and then.

Nat smiled to herself. Rob was very good – and even Gerald had had his moments – but all the porn she'd ever used had been of women. Women – degraded. Tied up. In bondage play or overtly sexual, all assets on display or as near has. Women –

She shook her head. 'You change the art in here every time I visit.'

Douglas smiled, gesturing to one of the comfortable leather chairs at the low table. 'Can I get you anything to drink?'

'I wouldn't mind a lemonade. Or a coke. I'm not a big drinker.'

Douglas fetched a glass and a bottle of lemonade. 'Ice?'

Nat nodded.

'How did you find the cider?'

'Cider?' Nat frowned. 'Oh, from the festival.' She nodded. 'It was nice. A bit sweet, but in small glasses it was good.'

Douglas gave her the glass, poured himself the same and sat down opposite her. 'It was about Clovis I wanted to talk, Nat. Mostly, Clovis.' He smiled, raising his glass.

Nat nodded, taking a mouthful of the cool lemonade. 'You want me to,' she havered.

Douglas nodded. 'It is,' he hesitated. 'I am building in – insurance, so to speak.' He held up his hand to forestall her. 'All being well, I will be around for thirty or more years. But Clovis is the issue.'

Nat raised an eyebrow.

'I have tried.' Douglas put his glass down. 'I paid for the best education I could for him. But,' he sighed. 'He, himself, I think, knows he wants to do more, but there is just,' he paused again. 'A disconnect. It was my idea to give him something to look forwards to.' He frowned. 'Not that that is quite right –'

Nat giggled. 'You're paying for him to have an escort.'

Douglas nodded. 'Yes. I want Clovis to understand the value of – earning – something. Of being respectable.'

'Respectable?'

'Maybe I worded that badly. I meant –'

Nat chuckled. 'I think I know what you meant, Douglas.' She blushed, ever so slightly. 'You wanted your son to have something to look forward to, if he earned it.'

Douglas nodded.

'And you want me to decide if he's earned it?'

Douglas nodded. 'I do. Bear with me while I explain –'

'I'm quite happy to do it,' Nat interrupted, surprising herself.

Douglas smiled. 'I'm so glad. Thank you, Natalayiana.' He smiled, the caution slipping from his face. 'There is – legal paperwork – to go with it. Clovis knows – he is not ready.'

Nat nodded. 'Yes, but your son and I,' she hesitated, not wanting to tell Douglas the whole disgusting truth of their relationship.

'I know, at university, you and he –'

'We were not quite lovers,' Nat gritted her teeth at the memory. Still, it had led to her meeting Robyn, so there were some strong positives to come out of it.

'I do not – particularly if it is a painful memory –'

'Your son's predilections were,' Nat shook her head, forcing herself to breathe out slowly. 'No. Rob asked him to come round, just before Christmas. I was unwell. He was a perfect gentleman. And before that, with Gerald,' she looked away, taking a mouthful of the lemonade. 'He can be perfectly honourable.'

Douglas nodded. 'I know. But,' he shook his head. 'Maybe it is Vic's death, but I want to ensure Clovis will be looked after – should the worst happen.'

Nat stared. 'Is there any reason to expect – anything?'

Douglas shook his head. 'None. Trust me. But I do not want to wait until – anything happens. I want you, Nat,' and his smile became cautious, 'Clovis has agreed to you becoming his – legal guardian.'

Nat stared. 'What?'

Lord Merryweather drew a large envelope up and laid it on the table between them. 'All the paperwork is in here. I suggest you take it away and read it. If you agree to it, sign it.' He smiled. 'Clovis has agreed to you becoming his legal guardian. He will have no assets to speak of, everything – if anything happens to me – will be his, but you will be the controlling agent. He will have no right to give anything away, to buy anything.'

Nat narrowed her gaze. 'You're worried – he'll be taken advantage of?'

Lord Merryweather nodded. 'I am. Technically, if anything were to happen, the property and assets remain his since you would be the guardian of them. He would have no assets unless you gave them to him.' He sighed. 'And that is something you might want to think carefully about, Nat.'

Nat stared. 'It's – an awful lot of responsibility. If anything happened, I could –'

'But you wouldn't, would you? You would do the right thing.'

Nat nodded. 'I cannot just – sign this.'

Lord Merryweather nodded. 'I do not expect you to, Nat. Read it closely. Discuss it with Rob, with your friend Robyn, anyone you trust. But there's more.'

'More?' she took another sip of her drink.

Douglas nodded. 'Acting as Clovis' legal guardian,' he paused, humour glinting in his eyes, 'technically you would be employed by the estate, and as such, there is a separate contract of employment and a wage schedule.'

'What?' Nat stared, wide eyed. 'I – I work for SHiP.'

Douglas nodded. 'Yes. And whilst I remain alive and sane,' he grinned, 'and trust me, I am entirely sane and serious about this – whilst it is payment, it is not much. If or when something happened to me, if you and I had not already thought Clovis had achieved a suitable level of – suitability, of comprehension – then it would rise significantly. At that point, dear Natalayiana, you would be running Merryweather Hall and Clovis would be your responsibility.'

Nat stared. Blinked.

'I.'

She blinked again.

'I.'

Douglas refreshed her drink.

'I.' She frowned. 'Why?'

He smiled. 'Because I trust you.'

--

Nat stared at Rob. 'He trusts me.'

Rob grinned. 'As well he should.'

Nat shook her head. 'No. I mean, if anything happens to him. Merryweather Hall becomes mine. Clovis becomes my responsibility.'

Rob stared open mouthed.

Nat shut his jaw.

'How – do you feel about that?'

Nat shook her head. 'For anything to happen, Douglas would have to be – gone. He's only sixty, there's years still. But he wants me to accept responsibility – including payment – for someone the same age as me.'

She shook her head, still stunned. 'I used to kneel before Clovis. He would masturbate onto my face, into my hair, my eyes.' She held her hand up to stop Rob's protestation. 'I knelt before him and his uni friends a number of times, naked, while they all masturbated over me.'

She looked up at Rob, smiling sweetly. 'Of course I'm going to do it.'

He swept her up into his embrace, hugging her. She put her hands on his shoulders, enjoying the warmth of his breath against her chest. He swept a hand down, drawing her skirt up, his hand on her bottom.

Nat felt her body tightening, enjoying the intimacy. She wrapped her legs around him, pulling the dress down on the left side. Rob nuzzled in, breathing heavily. Her eyes rolled back in her head as he bit down.

'Slowly,' she whispered.

She let him continue for a while before asking, 'Is Robyn coming round on Tuesday?'

Rob raised his head. 'I've got my mouth on your breast and you're asking about Robyn?'

Nat kissed him. Kissed him until his grip on her tightened once more.

'It's a big deal, Rob. Douglas wants me to be the responsible adult for Clovis. The man whose idea of a relationship was masturbating onto my face. Who liked getting his friends round so that half a dozen of them could masturbate over me.'

Rob set her down on the ground, slipping his arms loosely around her shoulders. 'Nat. Natalayiana. I love you. I think you should take this on. Not so you can get your own back on him, but so you can help him. Show him.'

Nat snorted. 'The first time we played tennis, he covered my chest in bruises.'

'And when I had to go out before Christmas and you weren't well, he was a perfect gentleman, you said.'

Nat nodded, almost absently. 'It's too much, Rob. Responsibility for Clovis – and Merryweather Hall.'

'If,' Rob stressed, 'anything happened to Lord Merryweather.'

Nat nodded, distracted. Douglas and Vic had been friends, good friends. Vic had been nineties, but they'd been friends for a long time. Are they the same age? Were they, I mean? Is Douglas older than he looks? Does he know something he's not telling me? Rob's people keep an eye on him, they think he knows someone who's a Were.

'I can ask Lucie and Gerald to come round, if you want.'

Nat looked up in surprise, frowning. 'Why?'

'I thought you might want to talk to Lucie.'

Nat stared. Blinked. It was too much to cope with. That level of trust. Responsibility. Merryweather Hall. And Clovis. And if anyone ever found out I was a Were – she managed to smile at Rob. I've got a wonderful boyfriend. A lord who trusts me to become the guardian of his son. Who entrusts his legacy to me.

But I'm – no one. A care worker. A junior care worker. If I'm not careful, if I get too excited, I turn into a Were-Squirrel. My body turns inside out. Bones break, muscles tear, ligaments tear. I like being disciplined. I love Rob. I like women. Not just Robyn – Laetitia as well. That convention woman – Nat blushed, remembering Daiandrea. Lucie.

I like – women in distress. I like being dominated by Rob. I like it when he tells me to go to work with no knickers on or nothing underneath my blouse.

I like sex.

Sex.

She looked up. The light was different in the room, Rob wasn't there. She looked around.

It's getting more physical with Rob. I *like* it getting more physical with Rob. Sooner or later he will take me out into the garden, undress me and lay me down for the neighbours to watch.

Nat blushed. I like the thought of making love to Rob in the back garden. But I couldn't do it.

I do like the thought – she blushed, furiously. I like the thought of Rob riding me, naked, in the back garden. Giving the neighbours something to watch.

She shook her head. No, I couldn't. I mustn't. I shouldn't.

Back at work tomorrow. She sighed. It had been a lovely week off, albeit with Vic's funeral. The new caseworker would have started at SHiP. Bryan had arranged a meeting with her for Monday morning – tomorrow.

A sound made her look up. Rob went past, smirking, swotting her bottom.

'Welcome back.'

He went to the front door and opened it; Lucie came in.

Nat blinked. 'What?'

Rob kissed her head. 'You were thinking so deeply I called Lucie. You were out of it, just stood there, mind adrift.'

Nat smiled at Lucie. Rob's sister was wearing a long grey robe, belted.

'I've got to go out, Nat,' Rob stroked her arm. 'Are you back?'

She stood on tiptoe and kissed him. 'I am. Thank you.'

He grinned, cupping and squeezing her rump. 'Don't know if I'll be back before tomorrow afternoon. Don't be late for work tomorrow.'

She stroked his arm and then he was gone. She smiled at Lucie.

'I don't know what –'

Lucie removed the belt and peeled the robe from her back. She was wearing pink underwear beneath it, frilly knickers and a camisole top.

'Rob said you wanted to talk. I thought you might like to look as well.'

Nat blushed.

Lucie peeled the straps of the camisole down, baring her breasts. 'Do you want to talk on the sofa or cuddle in your bed?'

Nat's blush deepened. She could still see the scars, faint lines, on Lucie's chest from where a previous boyfriend had torn her up. 'Won't Gerald –'

'Gerald's busy.' Lucie smiled. 'And he likes the thought of us being friends, maybe more.'

'You mean,' Nat smiled, shyly, 'he wants to watch us – together.'

Lucie nodded. 'We almost did, a while ago. But yes. He would like to watch the two of us make love. He thinks it would be – liberating – for you. And he knows I'd enjoy it.'

'I have,' Nat coloured, 'had sex with Robyn. You wouldn't be my first woman.'

Lucie chuckled. 'And you had a filthy weekend with Dr Gold. Rob said you liked being humiliated. And 69ing her.'

Nat flamed crimson. 'Your brother tells you – our secrets?'

Lucie laughed. 'Nat. You've got a healthy appetite and interest in men and women. There's nothing to be embarrassed about.'

Nat blushed. Managed to nod. 'I – I know. I was worried, when I told Rob, that I was bi, that he'd – leave me.'

Lucie smiled. 'I've had sex with several of Rob's girlfriends. Sometimes while he's watched, sometimes the two of us have shared a woman.'

Nat stared. 'The – two of you?'

'Yes. I like pussy. Particularly if it's not a girl who's bi. I'll eat her then sit on her face while Rob finishes her off. That way we both get boobs to play with.'

Nat blinked.

Lucie laughed. 'I am trying to shock you, Nat. Have I succeeded?'

Nat blushed, nodding.

Lucie pulled the camisole back up. 'Rob said you were – distracted? Overwhelmed?'

Nat nodded. 'Oh. Can I get you a drink of anything?'

'Tea, please.'

Nat went through to the kitchen, Lucie following her. 'I went to see Lord Merryweather. I'm not sure you've met him – oh. The winter festival.'

Lucie smiled. 'Fleetingly.'

Nat put the kettle on. 'He's drawn up a document. He wants me to be Clovis' legal guardian, in case anything happens to him.'

Lucie stared. 'Wow.'

Nat nodded. 'I know. Merryweather Hall, as well. Nothing will happen to him, obviously, and he'll change this at some point –'

Lucie hugged her briefly, tightly. 'You're not an imposter, Nat. You're good at your job. You're a decent human being.'

Nat hmphed.

Lucie pulled her round. Slapped her.

'Nat. You are human. Being a shape shifter doesn't make you less than human. You have *earned* Lord Merryweather's trust.'

Nat stared.

Lucie grinned. 'Nat. It is a big deal. But you are up to it. Don't put yourself down.'

Nat blushed. Rubbed her cheek.

Lucie laughed. 'I'm sorry, Nat. I might have struck you a bit forcefully. I'm as bad with Gerald. You both disbelieve yourselves when you've no reason to.'

'It's okay,' she smiled shyly. 'It is a lot to take in. The week off was lovely, but the last few days,' she shrugged, 'and I'm back at work tomorrow.'

Lucie pulled a face. 'We can take the teas upstairs and I can give you a massage, if you'd like.'

Nat smiled. 'I'd like that. If you don't mind.'

Lucie giggled. 'You would have to be naked. Of course I wouldn't mind.'

Nat blushed. 'It's been a long day. I wouldn't mind —' she hesitated.

'Ask.'

'I wouldn't mind – having a shower. If you wanted to join me.'

'You just want to see my boobs again.'

Nat blushed.

'Deny it?' Lucie grinned, raising an eyebrow.

Nat shook her head. She took a half step, put her arms around Lucie's waist. 'I don't deny it.' She kissed Lucie on the lips. She stepped back and gathered the skirt of her dress up. Drew it up, wriggling her hips until it was past them, then drew it up over her head.

Lucie stepped closer, wrapping her arms round Nat's waist and drew her into a kiss. 'You went to see Lord Merryweather with nothing but a half slip on under your dress.'

Nat grinned, pulling her shoulders back. 'I've got – nothing else – to cover.'

Lucie hooked her fingers into the hem of the slip and tugged it down. 'My, Nat. You are very hairy.'

Nat pulled Lucie in for a kiss but the woman pushed her away.

'Fair's fair.' She drew the camisole up over her head and discarded it.

Nat pulled Lucie back into her embrace, enjoying the feel of the other woman's breasts against her chest. Lucie ran her nails down Nat's back, making her gasp and shudder.

'You need a shower, a massage, and then a good ploughing.'

Nat slipped her fingers into the hem of Lucie's knickers. 'Promises, promises.'

Monday 4th April

'Come in, Nat, come in.'

Nat smiled, a little shyly, as she entered Bryan's office.

He shut the office door, still smiling. 'So, how was the week off?'

Nat nodded. 'It was good, thanks. We didn't really go anywhere. But there was Vic's funeral as well – he was a good friend of Lord Merryweather's –'

Bryan nodded absently. 'That's good, that's good.' He frowned. 'What did you say?'

'I was a guest of Lord Merryweather's at the funeral of one of his good – and oldest – friends.'

Bryan nodded slowly. 'Ah. Not so good. Sorry.' He shook his head. 'You've been off a week, Nat, and everything's changed.'

'I saw –'

Bryan nodded. 'The rebranding.' He shook his head. 'That wasn't my idea or wish.' He sighed. 'But Lord Merryweather provided funding last week, and a company he'd put me in touch with a while ago finally came through.' He smiled. 'That's where the money for the new caseworker came from.'

Nat nodded. 'How does that – what's my position? I was a caseworker.'

Bryan nodded, thin lipped. 'Yes, Nat, you were.' He sighed again. 'I like you, Nat. But as I've already said, you need to earn both my trust and George's trust.'

'I can never earn George's trust –' Nat protested.

'Why not?'

Nat stared, half tempted to tell her employer why, but knowing better than to do so.

Because someone sent his wife pictures of me naked from when I was in a cell, begging for Rob's and Gerald's lives. Because George's wife can't believe it wasn't me who sent them. Because she can't believe I *wouldn't* be having an affair with George. Because, mainly, she can't believe why anyone would send her photos of me naked unless they were trying to end George and my affair. She sighed. Except we hadn't been having an affair and I'd never thought of George that way.

'You see?' Bryan prodded. 'You need to re-earn our trust, Nat, and that's not happening, you're not telling us everything.'

'I need to earn – your trust?'

Bryan sighed. 'I know – you had issues with your last – boyfriend. I don't want to know the whole of it.' He scowled. 'But between – whysoever – that counsellor took against you, and whatever the whole truth might be, you're not – coming clean. You haven't explained all that you could.'

Nat stared. 'Bryan! You know me. I've worked for you – for years. I'm a very good caseworker. I shouldn't need –'

'You shouldn't, but you do,' he overruled her coldly. He stared at her coolly. 'You have two options, Natalayiana. You can walk out that door now, and I will give you a month's severance pay and a reasonable reference. Or you can suck up whatever issues you have, do your job, and earn mine and George's trust again. However long that takes.'

Nat stared. 'I've worked for you for years, Bryan.'

He nodded. 'Do you want to lose your job, Harewood? Are you a quitter?'

Nat scowled. 'No. You know I'm not. I'm very driven. I want to help –'

'And you will, Miss Harewood. You are an office assistant. Your pay will be reduced accordingly. I will still have you carry on interviews with some of our clients, but there will be additional office-based work for you.'

'But.' Nat stared, blinking hard, trying not to get annoyed, trying not to let her energy levels spike. 'You know George – doesn't like me. It'll be – awkward.'

Bryan nodded. 'I imagine it will be quite unpleasant at times, Nat. In my absence, you will report to George. He will allocate you work that he thinks fit for your – grade – if I am not around.'

'I can – take you to the tribunal.'

Bryan chuckled. 'How? I have not sacked you. If you wish to leave, I will give you a generous settlement. But I will not sack you, Nat.'

'But you want me to go.'

Bryan sighed. 'I don't, actually. You are a good office assistant, Nat. You might one day make it to being a caseworker again. But you have to earn it.'

--

'So this is your office junior?' Thomas looked her up and down. *Leered.* 'Short and scrawny. You some kind of hippie, Harewood?'

Nat stared, looking between him and Bryan.

'Nat,' Bryan spoke softly. 'Answer Thomas.'

Nat stared. 'Firstly, that's none of your business. Secondly, my height and weight are irrelevant. I'm perfectly capable –'

'But you're not, are you? You wouldn't have been demoted.' Thomas gloated. 'Was it your time of the month? Were you distracted? Trying to remember what shopping to buy to cook your boyfriend's dinner?'

Nat stared. Wheeled on Bryan. 'Bryan, you cannot let a member of your staff –'

'Answer the question, Miss Harewood.' Bryan spoke coldly. 'Remember your new position.'

Nat turned back to Thomas, trying not to seethe. 'No, it was not my time of the month. The night before the hearing, my fiancée raped me. He held me face down on the bed and had his way with me. When he was done, he walked out on me, left me bleeding and unconscious.'

Thomas shook his head. 'I'm sorry if you think it was rape, but he was your fiancée. You wanted to spend the rest of your life with him. Did you call the Police?'

Nat stared, feeling goose bumps rise on her skin, feeling anger wash through her.

Resist. He's just bating you. Testing you. He wants to make you mad. Wants to give Bryan a reason to sack you, to dismiss you with nothing.

'No,' she answered coldly. 'I – I still had feelings for him.'

Thomas shrugged. 'There you go. You still liked him. You didn't call the Police. You just didn't like being dominated, when you should be used to it.'

Nat stared, her fury waging war against her incomprehension. Why is Bryan not reining Thomas is? Is it a test for me – or him?

Thomas stared at her chest. Narrowed his gaze.

'For the next week, at least, you will be our receptionist. Marianne is on leave.'

Thomas turned to Bryan. 'I am not happy, Bryan, that our public face will be sitting out there. Bra-less.'

Nat stared. 'What?'

'Is it true, Nat?' Bryan asked, holding her gaze.

For that, nothing else, she felt a little bit of respect for Bryan. He was always – mercurial, but with Thomas – 'it's not really –'

'We are a professional company,' Thomas said to Bryan. 'How do you think it will look if a customer – or worse, a stakeholder – comes in, and our receptionist is sitting there, looking sluttish, hard nipples visible through her thin top.'

Nat stared. 'That's not really –'

'Well, Nat?' Bryan repeated.

Nat looked down. Raised her gaze. 'They're not visible. It's no one's business –'

'But every guest, every visitor, will see you sitting there, obviously braless. What sort of image do you think that will create, Miss Harewood?'

Nat stared, speechless.

'From tomorrow, Miss Harewood,' Bryan spoke coldly, 'please do not wear such a revealing dress. And, at least, wear a slip beneath it. Show some decorum.'

Nat stared speechlessly.

'I believe,' Thomas said, smiling tightly, 'you need to get to the reception desk?'

'We,' Nat blinked. 'We don't encourage guests, at SHiP.'

Thomas chuckled. 'There is a difference between our clients and stakeholders. Besides, the programme has changed. Get with it, Miss Harewood.' He nodded to Bryan. 'Now then, I have people to go and talk to. These files,' and he swept three files up off what had been her desk, 'won't prep themselves.'

'Bryan?' Nat asked, once the outer door closed behind him. 'What's going on?'

Bryan looked at her coldly. 'Your place is on the reception this week, Nat.'

'My desk –'

'You're on the reception. You don't need it this week.'

Nat turned on her heel and walked out of the office.

--

Nat looked up from the reception counter as the door opened, and her heart sank. 'George.'

George didn't even look at her as he headed in. 'Harewood.'

I can't blame – but what is *wrong* with Thomas? Why does he think he can talk like that? And why didn't Bryan interrupt him. Unless. She frowned.

'Harewood.'

Nat looked up. Bryan stood in the doorway.

'Attend me.'

'But the counter –'

Bryan turned on his heel and walked away. Nat scurried after him.

'Shut the door,' he said, when they were in his office.

Nat obliged, before sitting in the indicated chair.

'I've cut your pay by ten percent, Nat. You'll be on reception this week. Marianne should be back next week, but even if she isn't, there's some initial interviews I need you to carry out.'

'Ten percent? And my desk –'

Bryan sighed, looking at her and shaking his head. 'Your desk is a really minor issue, Nat.' He scowled. 'This is not the SHiP of two weeks ago.'

'Where does Thomas get off –'

Bryan held up his hand to stop her. 'We are still the Single, Homeless, integrated Project. But we are affiliated with Were Legal Opportunities. They have funded the rebranding, given us some clients and paid for Thomas.'

'So Thomas is one of them?'

Bryan raised an eyebrow. 'Thomas works for SHiP, as you work for SHiP, Natalayiana. Make no mistake on that.'

'But the things he was saying —'

Bryan shook his head. 'He works for SHiP. He is your colleague.'

'But you would never —'

'Harewood,' Bryan snapped.

Nat froze.

'Nat. Please. I am trying to explain. Lord Merryweather put me in touch with Were Legal Opportunities a number of months ago. I have been negotiating with them for a while. Thomas is a direct recruitment because of their funding.'

'But his attitudes —' Nat couldn't help herself.

'As part of Were Legal Opportunities, we have a broader remit, to support any Weres who come to be supported by them. Our work with the Independent Tribunal Service will continue, Natalayiana, and you may be part of that again one day.' Bryan sat back in his chair. 'Behind the scenes, Weres are — big business.'

'They're not,' Nat protested.

'They are,' Bryan answered softly. 'There are rumours of legislation being enacted or removed. Weres have been protected and are under threat.'

Nat tried not to shiver. 'But Weres,' she protested, to give herself time to think.

Rob might know more. The government knows Weres are real, they have their own – I don't know quite what it is. Anti-terrorism Were squad? They *know* Weres are real. This can't happen. They wouldn't abandon their own people, surely?

'They exist. They must exist.' Bryan shook his head. 'And we are in the perfect position, grass roots level, to see if we can find any.' He held his hands up to stop any response. 'They are not like that other company, H4W. Were Legal Opportunities have no wish to lock Weres up or put them into homes. They simply want to support them living their regular lives.'

Nat shook her head.

'Nat.' Bryan spoke coldly.

Nat matched his gaze.

'Thomas' attitudes –' he hesitated. 'Time and experience will soften him. He is arrogant, yes. He is also young.'

'Did this – they – Were Legal Opportunities – order you to employ him?'

Bryan shook his head. 'That is not your concern, Nat. Now then, I believe you are still seeing Jezabel Jones?'

Nat nodded. 'I'm not – seeing – seeing, but I'm still visiting her most weeks. In my own time.'

'Good, good.' Bryan nodded. 'Well, I won't keep you from the reception.'

--

'Come in.'

Nat smiled at Jezabel. 'You're looking – happy.'

Jezabel blushed. The flat smelled clean and fresh, and three walls were blank, stripped of the hideously bright orange wallpaper. It remained on one wall; the opposite wall had a number of pictures on it, including a couple of Jezabel from when she'd been a model.

'I'm really – looking forwards to – that convention.' Jezabel smiled timidly. 'You can still make it?'

Nat nodded. 'Furry by Nature? Yes, I'm looking forward to it as well.'

'Are you going to – dress up? It's a furry convention.'

Nat blushed. 'I might – not. I haven't decided.'

'Oh.'

'It's okay,' Nat smiled, touching Jezabel's arm briefly. 'You can. I want you to.'

Jezabel broke into a wide smile. 'Good. Because I've got – something to wear. Will you – stay, while I change into it. I want your opinion.'

Nat grinned. 'Of course.'

Jezabel hurried through to the bedroom. Nat took a seat, sighing softly. She couldn't remember her partner – a bimbo, she thought – but Daiandrea, the organiser, had sent her a pair of tickets to attend for free.

Once she'd explained her idea to Jezabel, the woman had gone for it. The chance to dress up, as a furry, in near-total coverage, so that no one would see her scars. The potential for Jezabel to have fun – in public.

Have I raised Jezabel's hopes too high? She thinks she'll meet someone, or at least have an encounter. She smiled to herself, thinking how enjoyable it might be to encounter Daiandrea. The only drawback was she'd only been able to get one hotel room for the pair of them, and that with a queen size bed. If Jezabel meets anyone and wants to bring them back –

If *I* meet Daiandrea and anything happens – she licked her lips at the thought of having an encounter with her. Dr Gold had been mesmerising, but Daiandrea had been something else altogether. Enticing. Younger than her, but very confident, much more confident than she was. There was something else about her as well, a musk, a scent, not of a Were – exactly – but *something*.

Something that Nat wanted to explore. She remembered the image that had come to her, lying flat on her back, Daiandrea rubbing her belly with her foot. To be in that position would be –

The door opened and Jezabel returned.

Nat stared.

Jezabel was wearing a skin-tight furry costume that emphasised her chest. A large tail was visible behind her: she waggled her hips and the tail wobbled. She wore a red-brown wig, which included a large pair of furry ears.

'A squirrel?' Nat asked, trying not to frown.

Jezabel nodded, smiling broadly.

Is that how I look? I will have to ask Rob to take some photos of me when I'm changed. 'How is the tail fixed?' she asked, moving round Jezabel to examine it.

Jezabel grinned, wriggling her hips again. 'It's a butt plug. Quite a large one.'

Nat blushed. 'Why does it look like,' she began.

'It's a squirrel wearing a thong.' Jezabel smirked. 'And if you peel the thong back, there's a zip. Full access.' The smirk dropped from her face. 'I should be able to find – someone – to bend me over something. The bodice amplifies and covers my tits – there's no zip for access to them – so all anyone can do is feel them up, not see the scars on them.'

Nat nodded absently. 'I can see why – you would go for it. And you're comfortable wearing it – in public?'

'I wouldn't change into it until we're in the hotel. And I do think of it as my first step.'

'First step?'

Jezabel sighed. 'I want to be like you.'

'Me?' Nat widened her eyes. 'Demoted, denigrated at work. Called a slut.' She gestured at her chest. 'One of my supposed co-workers was offended by me wearing a V cut dress and reckoned he could see my nipples; had the boss tell me off for being bra-less.'

Jezabel blinked. 'What?'

Nat nodded, sighing. 'New co-worker. Something's going on, but I don't know what. I think there's been some kind of deal done; the company's getting money to employ this person.'

'SHiP?'

Nat nodded again.

Jezabel stepped closer and wrapped her arms around Nat, squeezing her tightly. 'You're too good for them, Nat.' She rubbed her chest against Nat's. 'If anyone pulls me and wants more than a quick shag, they'll be very disappointed when I take the costume off. My tits are nowhere near this big.'

Nat pulled a face. 'At least you've got tits. I was still hoping when I was seventeen that I'd develop some; that I was just a late developer.'

Jezabel moved her hands down to Nat's hips. 'You've got hips, though. There's a nice swing to them.' She smiled shyly. 'I'm not trying to come onto you or anything, but you've got a nice backside. Curvy without being large.'

Nat blushed. 'Thank you.'

'I bet your boyfriend enjoys it.'

Nat blushed even more furiously.

'Does he put you over the end of the bed and have his way with you?'

Nat flamed crimson. 'Sometimes. He doesn't say anything, but I know all his exes are curvy.'

'But it's you he's with.' Jezabel smiled. 'I'm talking you up?' She chuckled. 'Thank you, Nat. You've done so much for me.' Her smiled faded. 'It's still difficult. But I look forward to your visits. I've started putting pictures – even of me – on the walls. There's the furry convention in a few weeks.' She grinned. 'It would be nice to get – something – there.'

Nat snorted. 'Don't,' she shook her head. 'It's a big step, Jezabel, even going out. And going out as that,' she forced herself to grin. 'Enjoy it for being out and about. You don't need to hope for anything more, as first steps go, it's a big one.'

Jezabel nodded slowly. 'I know. And,' she sighed. 'I'm hoping for more, because if I'm looking around, I won't realise – I'm out. In public. But,' she shrugged.

Nat nodded. 'That's a good way of looking at it. It is a big step. And I do hope you're not – disappointed.'

'Thank you.' Jezabel smiled shyly, wiggling her hips and making the tail waggle. 'I'll just go and change out of this. It is quite heavy.'

Nat nodded, watching her go through to her bedroom. Is it meant to be a Were onesie? A Were-Squirrel onesie? She shook her head. Or is it just a squirrel, sexualised? She snorted. I wonder what Rob would make of it. If other Weres have seen them. She shook her head again. I could hide in plain sight in one of them. I could make a mockery of what I am in one of them.

She looked away, tears pricking her eyes. Is the condition of being Were now up for mocking by the furry community, or are they allied? Are we a joke or – she sighed.

Work was shit, she accepted. I'm tired. Robyn's round tomorrow, she doesn't know – and, as much as I'm looking forwards to – the three of us – I'm worried how it'll change my relationship with Rob. And Robyn.

Tuesday 5th April

'You're a stubborn one.'

'Stubborn?' Nat asked, raising an eyebrow. 'Why do you call me stubborn, George?'

He snorted, scowling, barely looking at her. 'Don't you realise Bryan doesn't want you here? You're –' he shook his head. 'Deluded is being incredibly polite. You were a caseworker, once. Now you're an office junior. You won't ever be a caseworker again. Bryan has offered you a reasonable payout to go, and you remain. You're. Not. Wanted. Nat. Fuck off.'

Nat scowled, shaking her head. 'No, George. You can't speak to a colleague like that.'

He laughed, actually looking at her. He looked grey. Worn. There were rings under his eyes and he was unshaven. 'Because of you, or some mythical I don't know what, Evie and I are no longer together. Why the fuck would you send pictures of yourself to my wife, Nat, other than you were deluded and desperate? Why the fuck would anyone else do it, what would they gain from it?'

'I don't know.' Nat shook her head. 'Rob's looking into it. His department investigated –'

'Oh, your boyfriend's secret government department.' George shook his head. 'Deluded. Deluded.'

'George,' Nat begged. 'Please believe me. I didn't do it. Why would I do it? Why would I want you or Evie to know what I look like naked? I'm not trying anything.'

George shook his head. 'I thought you had something once, Harewood.' He moved past her and pushed the door open, going into the office.

Nat sat back down on the stool. She thought Bryan was already in; Thomas as well. She could hear voices from the office, but didn't try and hear who it was.

Is it time to move on? Lord Merryweather's offer would give me a little income; we could survive with Rob's money for a while, while I found something else. Bryan – blows hot and cold. George hates me. Marianne's off for a week, I've no support here. And Thomas – she shook her head, sighing.

The door opened and she looked up: Thomas strolled into the reception.

'So, Natalayiana.' He smiled tightly. 'It's good to see you dressed properly today. Where does the name Natalayiana come from? Eastern Europe?'

Nat scowled. 'My parents named me. Harewood is an old family name, Anglo Saxon times.'

He smiled falsely. 'And you're not interested in why they named you Natalayiana? You never asked them?'

'They're dead. Suicide, a number of years ago.'

Thomas stood blinking at her, like a fish out of water.

'Tell me about Were Legal Opportunities. Bryan said you were employed by them.'

'I'm not, I don't know,' he faltered. Narrowed his gaze. 'Very clever, Harewood. Were Legal Opportunities –

I believe – could use someone like you. You're cleverer than you look. You take instruction well.'

Nat snorted. 'What are Were Legal Opportunities up to? What's their raison d'être?'

Thomas smiled thinly. 'Everyone – even Weres – should have the legal right to do what they want, as long as it's within the law. Did you know Weres have to declare themselves as Were? That if a Were is discovered, not having declared themselves, it is a crime.'

'And I'm sure, declaring themselves as a Were, is only beneficial.'

'Of course it is. True,' Thomas smiled tightly, 'there is a possibility they might be discriminated against. But that is what Were Legal Opportunities are about. They exist to support Weres. But it's difficult to support those who don't come forwards.'

'Maybe they're afraid, if they come forwards, that their lives will be worse off. That they'll be given the equivalent of a yellow star to wear.'

Thomas snorted. 'That's hardly the case. Why would anyone care?'

'Fear?' Nat shook her head. 'People are afraid of what they don't know. Weres are the great unknown. There's legislation to protect them. Rumours that some were involved in the second world war. But no one's stood up and said they're a Were. No celebrity, no superstar, no sportsman. No one.'

'Pish.' Thomas waved his hand disparagingly. 'I'm sure, behind the scenes they must have. Legislation wouldn't just be enacted to protect a non-existent group of people.'

'Behind the scenes doesn't help. Without someone – or several – coming clean about being Were, they will always be – feared. Misjudged.'

'And what would you know about being a Were, Miss Harewood? Or was your boyfriend, the one who had rough sex with you, the one you wouldn't report, was he a Were?'

'It was rape.' Nat spoke calmly. 'It wasn't rough sex. There's a difference, Thomas.'

'Was he a Were, Nat? Was that why you didn't report him? Are you protecting a rapist, Nat?'

Nat stared. 'What?'

Thomas shook his head. 'You shouldn't be protecting someone who could hurt other people, Nat. He obviously didn't really hurt you, but he could hurt another.'

'Didn't. Hurt. Me?' Nat stared. 'Do you even know –'

'Nat.' Bryan spoke quietly, standing in the doorway.

Nat looked at him.

'Have you finished working on those files I gave you?'

'Almost. But Thomas –'

'Finish them.'

--

Nat unlocked the door wearily and let herself in. She could scent, straight away, that Robyn was in: both the smell of her, reassuringly female, and the scent of her milk. She opened the sitting room door and smiled: Robyn was sat on the sofa, legs stretched out, nursing Mildred. The blue blouse she wore was pulled open, revealing her braless state: her breasts hung heavy and full. Mildred gurgled and suckled noisily.

'Rob will be home soon.'

Robyn chuckled. 'My face is up here, Nat.'

Nat smiled wearily. She came round and kissed Robyn on the head, stroking baby Mildred's cheek. Baby Mildred wasn't that small anymore: she was nine months or thereabouts, a wriggler, and long-limbed.

Robyn slipped an arm around her waist, caressing her cheek. 'She's almost finished; would you like to have a hold of her?'

Nat nodded. She sat on the sofa next to Robyn, almost absentmindedly stroking her friend's belly.

Robyn eased Mildred from her breast and sat up, offering her daughter to Nat. Nat took her, cradling and cuddling her. Robyn lay back down again, sprawling languorously.

Nat cradled Mildred in her arms. The girl was almost asleep, a contented look on her face. She rocked her softly, knowing Mildred was as close as she would get to having a daughter of her own. 'She's beautiful,' she murmured.

Robyn chuckled. Nat glanced at Robyn. Her friend was sprawling decorously, arms crossed under her breasts. Even just spending two or three days with them a week was making her look fitter and healthier, giving her a warm glow, knowing Nat was standing between her and Dr. Gold.

'Nat,' Robyn's voice was almost a purr, 'my breasts are full and heavy. A tired office worker could lay herself down and have a full breast of milk.'

Nat adjusted Mildred in her arms, ensuring she was comfortable. The girl dribbled, eyes closing.

Holding her one armed, Nat reached out and laid her hand on Robyn's breast, stroking it softly, caressing her nipple. 'I did want to talk to you. While Rob wasn't here.'

Robyn smiled, eyes half closing. 'Talk away. Just keep stroking.'

Nat smiled, feeling the moisture under her thumb. 'Rob's agreed – to the three of us. Having some fun.'

She looked at the ripe, lush breast, not wanting to look at Robyn's face in case the offer no longer stood. She could see the tan lines running across the top of Robyn's chest but not lower, not as far down as she would have expected. 'You've not – sunbathed nude – for a while?'

'You can see I haven't,' Robyn answered softly. 'The sun comes quite strongly into my flat. You should come round one afternoon next week, if it's sunny. We'll sunbathe nude, the pair of us, in my sitting room.'

Nat blushed, removing her hand and adjusting Mildred's position in her arms. She was aware of Robyn sitting up, and then the woman wrapped her arms around her and Mildred.

'I'm going to be dribbling down your back,' Robyn breathed, nibbling at her ear. 'Tell me what you want to do with Rob and I.'

Nat turned her head and kissed the tip of Robyn's nose. 'I need to know – if you want Rob to wear a condom. Presuming, of course, that you're happy with – penetration.'

Robyn chuckled, stroking her daughter's thin hair. 'Rob fucks you regularly without a condom?'

Nat nodded.

'That's good enough for me.' Robyn chuckled. 'I want him to watch while you and I have fun.'

Nat nodded. 'I've already told Rob – if you said yes – he'd get to watch us together.'

Robyn pressed her chest against Nat's back. 'And I want him all to myself once, while you watch.'

Nat nodded, feeling the milk trickle down her back. 'I want to watch the pair of you together.'

'And I have something I want.'

'What?' Nat smiled. 'Name it.'

Robyn chuckled. 'After Rob and I have fucked, I want you.'

'I've got no –'

Robyn chuckled. 'I've not got to what I want.' She slipped her hand round Nat's waist, stroking her low on the belly. 'Once I've had Rob, and I've had you, and you're lying in my embrace,' she sniggered. 'I want to watch Rob filling your arse. I want to watch – and feel – him fuck your backside you while we're wrapped tightly around each other.'

Nat blushed. 'We've not – I've let him put a finger up there.'

Robyn chuckled, moving her hand to stroke Nat's chest. 'That's a start.' She grinned. 'What are your plans for Saturday?'

'I've got nothing specific –' she squeaked as Robyn pinched her nipple.

'A slip and a shirt? That's unlike you, Nat.'

Nat looked down at Mildred. Robyn's daughter was asleep. She rocked her gently.

'Bad day at the office?' Robyn asked, nibbling her neck. 'And here I kneel, braless, with two really heavy boobs.'

Nat blushed. 'Rob will be home soon.'

As she said it, she heard the key in the lock. She stared for a moment, longingly, at Robyn's breast. Her friend's body had always intoxicated her, and motherhood had only increased its appeal.

But Rob – Rob knew she was interested in Robyn and she had deliberately held back, not wanting to do anything without Rob knowing.

The door opened and Rob came in, grinning.

'Evening, both.'

He came and knelt before her. Nat looked up from Mildred, aware she was blushing slightly. Rob leant in and kissed her gently, his arm around her shoulders. Nat let him kiss her, fumbling the kiss awkwardly, more aware of Mildred in her arms.

'I should – put her down.'

Rob nodded, his eyes aglow.

Nat moved carefully, laying Mildred down into her cot. 'Are you free on Saturday, Rob?'

'Nothing that can't be rearranged. What had you in mind?'

She glanced at Robyn. Crossed back to Rob and knelt down, kissing him firmly, kissing him until his tongue was in her mouth and hers in his; until his hand was on her hip. She broke the kiss reluctantly.

'Robyn will be joining us on Saturday.'

'Early afternoon,' Robyn interjected. 'I'll have lunch and feed Mildred, then get dressed for the occasion and come around.'

'Come being the operative word,' Nat smiled shyly.

Rob grinned broadly, kissing her quickly. 'What – boundaries?'

Robyn smiled. 'I'm happy with kissing. With tongues. Full penetration, bareback. Pussy and arse.' She glanced at Nat. 'I am looking forward to you taking Nat's arse.'

Rob looked at her. 'Are you happy – with all of that? With making your bottom – available?'

75

Nat nodded, shyly. 'Yes.' She blushed furiously. The thought of – she knew Robyn was far more experienced than she was, would never let anything – damaging – happen.

Rob kissed her again, hands on her cheeks, his tongue teasing her lips until she opened to him.

Robyn sat back on the sofa, drawing her blouse together under her breasts. 'I was just offering Nat – and you, Rob – a full breast of milk. It'll save me pumping them, later. That is always painful and leaves them sore.'

Nat blushed.

'I want to take a shower,' Rob smiled meaningfully, 'but I think you should help your friend.'

'You don't mind?' Nat asked.

'You can have a breast-full as well, Rob,' said Robyn.

'No,' Rob shook his head. 'I don't mind. 'Why would I mind? It's not sexual. You're just – drinking your friend's milk.'

'And you?' Nat asked. 'I don't mind.'

'Ah,' Rob shook his head. 'It would be – strange. After Saturday, or maybe part of Saturday,' he flustered.

'Are you embarrassed, Rob?' Nat asked, smiling sweetly.

Rob nodded.

--

'I never thought you would be embarrassed by anything, Rob.'

Rob shook his head. 'It's an – odd thing. I get it's what boobs are for, it's natural, but,' he hesitated.

'But not for you?'

Rob nodded. Nat stroked his arm. Chuckled. She snuggled up closer, head on his shoulder.

'And you're okay with Saturday?'

Rob stroked her hair. 'Of course I am. It'll be fun.'

Nat snorted. 'That reminds me.' She lifted her head. 'I went to see Jezabel earlier. She's got this costume.'

'I'm not sure I want to know.'

Nat rolled her eyes. 'It's of a Were Squirrel. Furry, big bushy tail, the works.'

Rob frowned. 'The furry market is a surprisingly large one.'

'But of Weres?'

Rob shrugged. 'There's a lot of crossover. If there's no Weres in the public eye, how can the costume be a rip off of one? It – kinda sucks, if the furry community is making fun of Weres, but,' he sighed, stroking her head again. 'It could just be one manufacturer. It could be the easiest thing they had to convert to make it.'

Nat frowned. 'It still felt – wrong. Dressing up as Weres, whether it's a rip off of a Were or not. It's like dressing up as a woman, or a black man, for a laugh.'

Rob shrugged. 'If you can find a label, I can look around. It's a bit out of the department's jurisdiction.'

Nat shook her head. 'That wasn't why I raised it, Rob.' She sat up. 'SHiP's – it's changed. We're now affiliated with – what was it? Were Legal Opportunities.' She frowned. 'There's a new caseworker. Thomas,' she scowled.

'Not up to the job?'

She shrugged. 'I don't know. He seems to revel in putting me down, being rude, telling me I dress too salaciously, that it,' she shook her head, veering away from what she'd been going to say. 'And Bryan seems to be in his pocket. I think this Were Legal company put money into SHiP.'

Rob nodded. 'That's what Bryan wanted from Lord Merryweather, isn't it?'

Nat nodded. 'But there's a whole rebranding and Thomas,' she frowned.

'Thomas what?'

'I think they want Weres made public. Then they'd have a job, defending them.'

Rob snorted. 'Dangerous. Did you know you were vetted, Nat?'

Nat stared. 'What?'

'Because we are going out.' He half grinned.

'And if they'd found anything in my background?'

Rob shook his head. 'The department wants,' he hesitated, frowning. 'They want to know. It's like they want to know where any leaks might be, or any issue, so they can plug them before they start.'

Nat scowled. 'I'd never reveal –'

'That's not what I meant.' He stroked her arm softly. 'The department use Weres. They are well aware

Weres are real. I don't know whether they want to be the only people who have Weres, or whether there's something else going on.'

'But you suspect them?'

Rob hesitated. 'They're a government department. Not to be trusted without checks. Not to be automatically believed. But.' He grinned. 'They do good work. Or try to. Linksfield is locked away indefinitely, without probation or early release. That site H4W had is secured against them and anyone else stumbling into it and using it. They routinely run checks to see if they can trace back that video feed.'

'Oh. You didn't tell me. I thought they'd done — nothing.'

Rob nodded. 'I didn't see the point of telling you unless or until they find something.'

Nat frowned. 'There was — someone at work mentioned it. A newspaper article about Mal and H4W. Something about him — stalking and kidnapping someone. Me.'

Rob shook his head. 'No. There was a total news blackout. Nothing local, nothing in the nationals, nothing on social media.'

Nat shook her head. 'It was — before Christmas. There were flowers — supposedly from Mal. They might have been from Jack.' She scowled, rubbing at her forehead. 'I think it was Bryan who mentioned that he'd read an article on Linskfield and H4W. He said he didn't have it anymore.'

'Do you want me to speak to Bryan?'

Nat looked up at Rob. 'My hero, riding in.' She smiled. 'No. I'll speak to him tomorrow.'

Rob settled back down, drawing her into his embrace. 'Anything to help you sleep?'

Wednesday 6th April

'Is Bryan in today, George, do you know?'

'How the fuck would I know, Harewood?' George spat viciously at her. 'Get back on reception and do your job. If you can.'

'George,' Thomas spoke calmly, looking up from what had been her desk, 'why has Nat earned your wrath?'

George scowled at her. 'She knows.'

'I asked a civil question, George. Bryan said –'

'I don't care what Bryan said,' George snapped, rounding on Thomas. 'This dumb bitch caused my wife to leave. She hates me. After twenty odd years –'

'I am the innocent party, George.' Nat spoke softly. 'I did nothing.'

'Nothing?' George yelled, rounding on her. 'Nothing!? Stupid bitch sent my wife –'

'I didn't,' Nat reiterated. 'Why would I? I wasn't having an affair with her or you. Why would I do it, George? Hmm?'

He looked at her furiously. Scowled. Shook his head. 'She's a liar. Tells half-truths. Paints herself as the victim.' He stared at her, hatred in his gaze.

'I've not lied about anything, George. Do you want me to tell you what it was like again, waking up naked and in a cage? Watching as a friend was shot. Another abused in front of me. Thinking I was going to be shot, raped, tortured?'

'When did this happen?' Thomas asked, coolly.

Nat looked at him. He seemed dispassionate. 'There was – is – a company called Homes for Weres. They wanted SHiP to work with them. One of their people kidnapped me. They wanted me to admit I was a Were, they tortured Rob and Gerald –'

George snarled and turned away.

Thomas shook his head. 'Are you a Were? That sounds like the sort of thing Were Legal Opportunities could represent you over.'

Nat shook her head. 'That's not the point of it.'

George turned, his cup in his hand. He tossed it at her and she caught it automatically.

'I've finished my coffee. *Nat.* Clean it and get me some water.'

Nat stared. 'I'm not a skivvy. I'm –'

'You're the office junior,' George finished. 'If you ever want a shot at caseworker, you've got to impress me. Impress me. Clean it. Get me some water.'

Nat stared. Looked at Thomas.

He shrugged. 'It's your chance, Harewood. Curry favour with George.'

Nat shook her head in disgust. If you're so shallow that cleaning your cup impresses you – she sighed under her breath. Poor Evie. I thought George was okay, once. She turned away. Seems I was so wrong.

She went through to the kitchen. The linoleum was faded, the light had lost its shade and there was a faint smell of burnt toast. She cleaned George's cup, scrubbing at the coffee ring. It was –

She clenched her teeth together.

It wasn't – it was – she scowled. Whatever Thomas' motive – and George's constant bad mood – she frowned. I doubt it would work, going round to see Evie. I don't even know if she's in their house or George is. What if I ask Rob to go round?

After a moment she shook her head. No. Ask my boyfriend – *boyfriend* – she blushed. The things Rob did for her – keeping her safe when she changed, doing the shopping if she was busy, ensuring the bills were paid – she grinned. Never mind the fact that some mornings it was difficult to get going, that she started some days sore and quite tender.

She sighed. Not long until Saturday. She blushed bright beetroot at the thought of being in bed with Robyn and Rob. To kiss her best friend in front of Rob. To share Robyn with Rob, fully. Robyn was coming round early afternoon; would hopefully spend the night with them.

Nat could feel the silken slip rubbing against her sensitive nipples. Stop thinking about fucking your lovers.

She blushed. Drew down a plastic cup, looked at the water machine.

Swallowed. It was empty. Normally it was Marianne – or George and her – who changed it. There was a new bottle, but it was heavy, awkward and too much for her on her own.

I cannot go out and ask anyone for help. George –
is this a test?

She took the empty bottle off the machine: that
was easy enough. Unscrewed the lid. It wasn't difficult to
do, she'd done it with George a number of times. It was
always a messy, wet, affair. Can I lift it on my own? She
crouched down next to it, sitting on her heels, and tried. It
was slippery and difficult to hold.

She stood up slowly. It was a straightforward
procedure. Lift the bottle. Balance it on the edge of the
machine. Tip the bottle upside down and ram the neck
into the hole of the machine.

She shook her head. 'I'm going to get soaked,' she
murmured.

Or I go and ask Thomas or George, tell them that I
can't do it on my own. She shuddered at the thought of
asking either of them for help.

Nat leaned down, grabbing hold of the bottle and
getting comfortable with it. A straightforward lift to the
edge of the machine. I don't want to take too long – it'll
strain my arms and the last thing I want is someone
walking in, wanting to know what's taking me so long.

She took a breath and lifted. It was heavy, heavier
than she'd imagined, and the plastic felt slippery in her
hands. The water jostled and rocked in the bottle,
threatening to spill over. Somehow, she managed to get
the bottle to rest on the lip of the machine.

Lift further, she thought, and flip – ha. Turn it so
it's pouring into the machine. Bring the bottle down on the

hole. Nothing to it. She could feel the strain in her arms and gritted her teeth.

I can do this. I'm stronger than I look.

She hefted, aware of the strain in her thighs as she pushed up, and then the bottle was turning, she was guiding it – as best she could – towards the hole. Water splashed across her belly and legs but it was going in.

The bottle went into position. Nat breathed a sigh of relief. The bottle rocked.

Nat took half a step. The bottle crashed –

Nat got her hands to it but it crashed into her, knocking her down, water flooding out. She hit the ground hard, the bottle on and between her legs, pouring across the floor. Nat grabbed at it –

'Nat.' Thomas sighed, holding the door open, shaking his head. 'You should have said something.'

She heard George's sigh even as she managed to grab the bottle, now half empty, and lift it the right way up.

'Oh, for fucks sake,' she heard George mutter as he stomped away again.

Thomas grabbed a towel and let it fall onto the sodden floor, before passing her the kitchen roll.

'Make sure it's all dry when you're done, Nat. And you'll need to order another bottle. And put that one back into the machine, I don't think George is too impressed.'

Nat scowled, looking up at him. 'Can you help me put the bottle in?' She gritted her teeth. 'Please.'

Thomas nodded. 'Of course. As soon as the floor's safe to walk on.'

--

'I feel like a fucking mermaid,' Nat moaned.

She'd had a hot shower on getting in, but had spent the afternoon damp, soggy and uncomfortable from the waist down. She'd put towels over the bed and stretched out upon in, naked, legs spread.

Rob lay almost upon her, his hands on her thighs, his head hovering about her hips. 'I've never known of a mermaid to be so hairy.' He grinned, ruffling her fur. 'It'd weigh heavy.' He stroked her thighs, leaning in to kiss her.

'You like me – hairy?' Nat asked, suddenly wondering if she should have spent years of her life shaving, plucking, pruning.

Rob laughed, kissing her again, his hands fondling her knees. 'I'm a Were, Nat. You're a Were. I like seeing your pelt on you, in human form.'

Nat blushed.

Rob moved his hand, caressing the thick fur between her legs. 'You could – go to the convention in a furry suit. No one would know.'

Nat shook her head. 'It's what Jezabel is wearing. I wouldn't want to – she fills out the costume much better than I ever would.'

Rob smiled, kissing her thigh. 'I bet she can't actually turn into a real squirrel though, if I got her too excited.'

Nat smiled. 'And if I get you too excited you become a big spikey hedgehog.' She looked at Rob meaningfully. 'I do want to get you too excited – soon. I want to see what I can do to – and with – you in Were form.'

Rob grinned, licking her lips.

Nat shivered. 'And you're okay with Saturday?'

Rob chuckled. 'Love, your best friend is coming round and we're having a threesome. What's not to be okay about?'

'I know I've changed – well, not *changed* – but changed since we started going out, Rob. You've given me confidence. I love you. I like women. I'm not wholly opposed to the idea of doing things – outside. I'd like to have another go at a puppy pile with Lucie and Gerald. I like the idea of a holiday cottage somewhere with them. I'm – really looking forwards to Saturday.'

Rob nodded. 'We should,' he hesitated.

Nat raised an eyebrow.

'I almost don't want to bring it up.'

Nat nodded. 'Robyn. And Weres.'

Rob nodded. 'If we – if I – have full penetrative sex with her –'

Nat sighed. Nodded. 'She is – breastfeeding. She might not –'

'I'd still be – fucking your best friend, Nat. And if Robyn did get pregnant.' He stroked her belly softly. 'I know – there's not much chance –'

Nat took his hand, raised it to her lips and kissed it. 'There's not much chance of her conceiving. But it's possible, realistically –' I see Robyn with Mildred. I want that. Family. Community. Kinship.

'How would you feel,' Rob asked, 'if Robyn was carrying my child?'

Nat sat up. Guided Rob's hand back between her legs. 'If I can't bear your child, I would rather Robyn did.'

Rob drew her into his embrace, kissing her passionately. Nat clung to him, feeling herself getting wetter and wetter.

Rob broke the kiss at last, easing her back down onto the bed. He pushed her knees apart further. 'Now then, since madam is presenting her delectable entrée, I should do the polite thing and tuck in.'

Nat giggled. It would be alright.

Thursday 7th April

Bryan gestured to the seat opposite his desk. 'Sit down, Nat.'

Nat sat.

Bryan sat down, sighing, pulling over a couple of printed documents. 'Have you had any contact with anyone at Oxford City Council or Oxfordshire Borough Council recently?'

Nat frowned, shaking her head. 'No. I used to meet their reps occasionally,' she trailed off.

'Oh?'

'When I was a caseworker. I met a number regularly.'

Bryan frowned. 'They were on the other side of the case.'

Nat nodded. 'Yes. But sometimes sharing information saved all parties time and effort. I surrendered no cases, I gave away nothing –'

Bryan waved his hand dismissively. 'I'm not talking about that. I've had people from both councils writing, asking if we can take on cases like that,' he clicked his fingers, trying to remember a name.

'Jezabel Jones?'

Bryan nodded. 'Yes. One of them praises your handling of the situation,' he scowled, 'whilst simultaneously confirming that as she's off their books there'll be no more payment but asking if they can send us more like that.'

Nat sat silent. Jezabel had come a long way – but it was slow and difficult, and failing to turn up one week could potentially undo everything she'd worked at for months. But Jezabel was up for going to the Furry convention and that was a big step forward. She still wouldn't go out on her own, but steps were being made.

'Didn't – Were Legal Opportunities – put some money into SHiP? Will that cover it?'

Bryan scowled, shaking his head. 'Yes, but that's not the point. They put money in for us to work with them, for our rebranding, and to get a new caseworker in. Thomas. The money from the council –'

'That's the council for you, Bryan. If I'd done – not so good a job – they'd have continued paying. Possibly. While Jezabel didn't improve in any way.'

Bryan scowled at her.

'The council can't have been paying that much.'

Bryan shook his head. 'It's not that. Why are both councils asking for you, and why now?'

Nat shook her head. 'I don't know. Obviously, my work with Jezabel tipped the scales with one council,' she shrugged. 'They do talk to each other.'

'Have you had any recent dealings with anyone from either of them? Or the Independent Tribunal Service?'

Nat shook her head. 'No.'

He stared at her for a moment, expecting her to say more.

Nat met his gaze, unspeaking.

'Next week,' Bryan said, eventually, 'I've got several clients lined up for you to go and interview. Most of next week you'll be out of the office.'

'I have no desk here, either.'

Bryan scowled. 'That's not really –'

A knock at the door interrupted him. Before he could say anything the door was opened –

'Natty!' Clovis exclaimed, beaming.

'Ah, Mr Merryweather,' Bryan began.

'Lord Merryweather,' Nat spoke formally, half rising.

Clovis seized her in a bear hug. 'Natty. I just wanted to check you hadn't forgotten about tonight?'

Nat shook her head. 'Of course I haven't, Clovis. I'll see you later.'

Clovis grinned. 'I'm looking forwards to this. Pa said he'd told you all of it.'

Nat nodded. 'He did. We'll go through it later, Clovis. I am working here –'

'Rubbish, Nat,' said Bryan, trying to smile, 'if you've got a meeting with Clo – I mean, Lord Merryweather, of course you've got to go.'

--

Nat looked around the austere room, trying not to frown. There was a table and two dining room chairs; only a small window, and the walls were painted a dull grey colour, the paint smelling fresh. One wall was dominated by a picture – Nat thinned her lips.

'What is this room?'

'Pa said you should have a room here. An office.' Clovis withdrew a ring with two keys on it; he'd used them to unlock the door. Passed them over.

'Did you have the room – repainted for me? Decorated?'

Clovis nodded enthusiastically. 'Yes. Do you like it?'

'I appreciate Douglas' thought,' Nat answered carefully. 'It may be quite useful. But the art –'

Clovis turned round to look at it. He'd given her the chair behind the desk; presumably, this was her office at Merryweather Hall when she was dealing with – him, or anything else.

'What's wrong with the art, Nat?'

Nat shook her head. 'Apart from not bringing any life or colour to the room, it shows a naked woman sat on the edge of a desk. There's a naked man in front of her, with his head in her lap.'

Clovis frowned. 'That's not – inappropriate? You said once you liked it when Rob did that for you.'

Nat stared. 'Clovis,' she spoke coldly, 'this meeting is about whether – this month – you have earned the right – to spend time with Felicita. It's not appropriate that you should put a piece of art, referencing,' she frowned. 'When did I say that?'

'Are you turned on, Nat? It was before Christmas last year. You weren't well. Rob asked me to look after you. You talked. Babbled. A lot.' He smiled. 'You said you liked it when Rob used his tongue on your clitoris.'

'Clovis, that is not appropriate. Anything I may have said, while I was – out of it –' she was aware she was blushing, that Clovis should bring up something like that –

'But we were lovers, once,' he said plaintively.

Nat sighed. 'Once. Over ten years ago, Clovis. It is not polite to talk about what a woman might like – or dislike – sexually, if you are not going out with her, or to anyone else.'

'But do you like the picture?' Clovis persisted. 'I thought it would be a happy memory, while you were here. Of Rob.'

Nat shook her head, fighting against her anger. 'I appreciate the thought, Clovis, but I don't want to be looking at the picture of a naked woman –'

'Would you rather it was a picture of you up there?'

Nat stared.

'It could be a picture of you now,' he began.

'Clovis, this is not –'

'Or there are those photos of you and I from uni days. I found them the other day.'

Nat stared. 'What? Who took them? Where?'

Clovis shrugged. 'It was in a bedroom. Mainly it was the other way round. You had your head in my lap.' He smiled. 'I always liked how you could get the whole of my cock into your mouth, even though it was big. It was always nice, feeling you lick it.'

Nat shuddered. 'Clovis, I want those photos. I do not want you to have them.'

He scowled. 'But it was nice, when you took me into your mouth.'

'After the funeral,' Nat said, 'what happened with Felicita? Did you take her – to your room?'

Clovis nodded, a smile breaking out on his face again. 'She let me look at her tits. She wouldn't let me touch them, but they are very nice.' He looked up at her and smiled innocently. 'You would probably like it if you had tits like hers. They are quite large.'

'This isn't helping, Clovis –'

'She put her hand down my trousers. She let me look while she touched.' He looked at her again, intently. 'I want to go further with her. I want to see her tits.'

Nat forced herself to smile, thinly. 'I think, particularly since you have already had time with her, and she – brought you pleasure – that you shouldn't be allowed a visit this time.' She sighed. 'Clovis, you know your – pa – has given me legal – authority – over you.'

Clovis nodded. 'I know.' He sighed. 'Nat,' he smiled awkwardly. 'I am trying, Nat. I painted the room myself. I thought it looked nice. Like an office. Then I thought it looked plain. So,' he waved his hand at the picture.

Nat nodded. 'I can see you're trying, Clovis. The room is nice, but the picture is unsuitable. Unless I specifically raise it, I would ask you not to mention anything about our – relationship – in university.'

Clovis seemed to deflate. 'Are you – embarrassed – by me?'

Nat frowned, shaking her head. 'No, Clovis, I'm not. But our relationship was not good. For either of us.'

'It was –'

Nat shook her head. 'I can remember, Clovis, kneeling naked before you. You were my first boyfriend. But you didn't want to fuck me or have me perform oral sex on you. You masturbated onto my face. You brought have a dozen of your friends in and you all wanked over my face, my hair, my chest, my back.'

Clovis had the grace to look apologetic. 'You've grown up, Nat,' he said awkwardly. 'Help me – grow up. Enough to – manage – Merryweather Hall.'

Nat frowned. Thoughts flitted through her mind, scattering and crumbling at Clovis' words. Lady of Merryweather Hall. A sanctuary for Weres. Large bedrooms where she could have Rob, Robyn, Lucie and even Gerald installed as near-permanent lovers. Not having to work for SHiP; not taking abuse from Thomas and George, from Bryan.

Rob kneeling before her, stimulating her. Lucie behind her, her tongue teasing Nat's arse. Robyn leaning over her, Nat's mouth full of soft breast and warm milk. Gerald sucking her chest, biting her nipples. Her hands full of cock and kitty.

Nat shook her head. It was a fantasy. Nothing more.

'Will you not – help me?'

Clovis looked downfallen. Like a big, useless, lump.

Nat sighed. 'Of course I will help you, Clovis.'

Part 2

Friday 8th April

'I don't want to go to work today,' Nat whined.

Rob scowled at her. 'None of that, Nat. Robyn will be round tomorrow. That'll give you something to look forward to.'

Nat sighed. 'It does. But I'll be stuck on the reception again, and if Bryan's in he'll have a go at me, and if he's not —'

'You're in the lobby area?' he asked.

Nat nodded. 'Yes. Thomas is just — I don't know what his problem is, other than he's an arsehole. And George is getting worse. Obviously trying to patch it up with Evie didn't work. There must have been —'

'So you'll not be in the main office, so can spend most of the day ignoring them.'

Nat scowled. 'Are you humouring me?'

Rob nodded. 'Yes. I know it feels shit there at the moment, but it's Friday. The end's in sight.'

Nat sighed. 'Are you looking forwards to shagging a woman with actual tits?'

Rob sighed. 'I'm looking forward to shagging the woman I love while another watches. I'm looking forwards to watching *you* shag Robyn, or maybe it'll be Robyn shagging you.'

'So you're thinking about Robyn and what she'll look like naked. What she'll taste like.'

Rob crossed his arms over his chest. 'Nat. I'm going to work now. If you want something to really feel self-pitying about, I'll roll you onto your belly, part your cheeks and drive myself, as hard as I am, up your arse.'

Nat stared, furious. And burst into tears.

Rob leaned over and drew her into his embrace, putting her in his lap. 'Nat. Take a day off work if you're not feeling it. After the way you've been treated,' and he kissed her head softly. 'I would never fuck you in rage, Nat. I am,' he stroked her gently, 'I am looking forwards to possibly exploring that part – of things – when Robyn's here. I want you to feel comfortable and ready for it.'

Nat whimpered, clinging to Rob.

He stroked her tenderly. 'We could go to the pictures later, if you wanted. Or anything.'

Nat leant in, kissing his neck. 'I do have an idea of what I might do.' She smiled softly. 'Will you manage all day,' she asked, mock-shyly, 'as hard as you are?'

Rob shook his head reluctantly. 'I should be going. By the time I've warmed you up –'

'I can – take you as I am,' Nat hesitated. 'Just unbutton your trousers and let me sit on you –'

Rob kissed her. Filled her mouth with his tongue. Had one hand upon her cheeks and with the other pinched and tweaked and tugged her nipple.

'I am not going to fuck you and leave you unsatisfied, Nat. Either I make you happy first or we hold off 'til later.'

Nat kissed him, murmuring in the back of her throat. 'One day I am going to tie you up tight, Robert Adams. I'm going to ride your face, your chest and your cock, see how much you can give me before I break you.'

Rob grinned. 'Make sure Lucie is nearby. I don't want to shift while you're riding me.'

He laid her back on the bed, sliding out from underneath her. Lifted her foot and kissed her ankle; licked her toes before grinning and heading out of the bedroom.

Nat sprawled. It was still early. She heard the front door open, Rob call out a farewell, and then the door closed on him softly. She sat up slowly, sliding her hand down until it rested on the thick mound of fur.

'Are all Weres this randy?' she wondered. 'I don't even know,' she shuddered. The conversation with Clovis. 'Can I cope with him?' She sighed. 'And there's SHiP. And Robyn,' she smiled shyly. 'I want to watch Rob with Robyn. Lucie said his type was busty women.' She drew her hands up her own flat chest. 'What does he see in me?'

She padded through to the bathroom, pausing to look at the full length mirror Rob had had installed. 'God I'm hairy,' she murmured, looking at the hirsute almost-boy in the mirror. 'Flat chest. At least I've got some curves.' She half turned to admire herself. It was nice, the few times Rob had put her over something and taken her from behind. Even just putting her over or against something and dry-humping her.

She shook her head slowly. 'You can do this. It's just work.'

Saturday 9th April

Nat hurried to open the door, fighting to hide her smile. Her *leer*. They'd lunched early. Shared a shower and managed to avoid fucking each other – somehow – both desperately horny and waiting for Robyn to arrive.

'Robyn,' she smiled, pulling the door open.

Robyn smiled wearily, juggling a wriggling, wailing, Mildred in one arm, a large leather bag in the other. Robyn passed her the leather bag and Nat took it, stepping back into the house.

'That's got – my toys,' Robyn smiled, her eyes tired. 'Mildred needs a good feed, then once she's asleep I need a shower and then I,' she smiled, her eyes gleaming. 'I'm looking forward to watching Rob as we fuck.'

She followed Nat in, rocking Mildred one-armed and pushing the door closed with her foot. 'I'm looking forward to fucking Rob as well.' She put Mildred down on the sofa, then leant in, kissing Nat quickly, dropping her hands to squeeze and fondle Nat's bottom.

Nat kissed Robyn, aware of the dampness on her chest. Robyn pulled back, grinning, as Rob entered the room.

'Rob,' Robyn went to him, kissing him, hugging him, pressing herself against him. She pulled back, grinning. 'Sorry. Feed my daughter first and get her to sleep, then it's a shower and then fun time.'

She smiled at both of them, unbuttoning and discarding her damp blouse. Pulled the left cup of her bra down, deliberately flashing Rob as well before bending down to pick her daughter up.

As Mildred latched on, suckling noisily, Robyn chuckled, sitting down carefully. 'So to recap,' she smiled at both of them, 'kissing is okay with both of you?'

Nat glanced at Rob; nodded, sitting on the arm of the sofa. 'We're okay with – everything.' She blushed. 'I'm okay with Rob – fucking you. I'm okay with him using his tongue, his fingers, anything, everything, on you.'

Robyn looked at Rob. 'And you're okay with me eating your lover's pussy? And with me sticking my tongue – or fingers – in either of your arseholes?'

Rob nodded without hesitation. 'I – we – are. I'm hoping – in a while – to take Nat's arse. I'd like her to be in your arms – before. And,' he hesitated, slightly awkwardly.

Robyn laughed. 'Nat, has Rob *still* not fucked that lovely arse of yours?'

Nat shook her head, blushing.

Mildred raised her head. Burbled. Burped, dribbling a little. Robyn cleaned it up without noticing. As she went to put her daughter down, Mildred latched on again.

'Arse, pussy and cock all round then.' She smiled. 'I've dribbled on both of your shirts. You might as well lose them.'

Nat stripped off her T shirt. Rob did a moment later and Robyn made a show of gazing at both of their chests. She grinned.

'Nat, have you knelt before Rob?'

Nat hesitated. 'Once only. That's –'

'No, that's not something we,' Rob began.

'Then you won't object if I kneel before him at some stage?'

Nat shook her head. 'No, of course, that's fine.'

Robyn chuckled. 'I'll be kneeling before you as well, Nat. I know why you don't kneel to Rob.'

'Yes,' Rob said, awkwardly.

'But you kneel before Nat?'

Rob nodded. 'Of course. I like having my tongue on or in Nat as she climaxes.'

Nat blushed. Robyn removed Mildred from her breast and laid her in her crib. Mildred burbled, her eyes closing contentedly.

Robyn chuckled. 'Rob, while I'm kneeling before you Nat will be teasing you – elsewhere – with her tongue. And while I'm eating her, you'll be teasing her with yours.'

Nat flared crimson.

Robyn laughed. 'I need a shower, otherwise I'd take you in my arms now and feed you Nat, making Rob lick your arse while I was at it.'

Nat looked at Rob, a little shyly. He looked at her, grinning.

Robyn stood up, leering at both of them. 'Give me five minutes once you hear the shower finish to get myself into position on your bed, then I'll call for you.'

She picked up her bag and headed upstairs. Rob crossed to her and wrapped his arms around her.

'You're shivering!'

Nat nodded. 'I'm scared. And excited.' She leaned in and kissed Rob and he held her, hands in her hair tilting her head back, exploring her mouth with his tongue.

At last they broke apart and he turned her round, pushing her over the back of the sofa.

'If Robyn wasn't here,' he whispered, running his hands down to her jean-clad bottom.

Nat wriggled. Rob pressed himself against her and she could feel his desire. He wrapped his arms around her, caressing her chest.

'If she wasn't here – but I want to watch you with her.'

He pinched her nipples and she chirruped in pleasure. He tightened his grip and she moaned. He tightened his grip again, just for an instant, making her gasp, before releasing her. She staggered; he caught her, wrapping his arms around her shoulders.

'How was yesterday? Or don't I want to ask?'

Nat shook her head. 'Let's just say, I'm looking forward to having things to bite. I'm going to be marking both of you.' She grinned. 'Robyn doesn't like having her boobs bitten – probably even more so now – but she's quite happy if you bite her arse.'

Rob chuckled, caressing her thighs. 'I am planning to bite you in quite a few places. And Robyn.' He kissed her again. 'I'm looking forward to Robyn eating you. And you eating Robyn.'

Nat smiled. 'So am I.' She blushed. 'It's been – a few minutes. I'll just go and – check.'

She scurried upstairs. Don't get excited. Don't get *too* turned on. Whatever else you do, *don't change!* She tapped on the door; gave it a moment.

'Robyn?' she asked, pushing the door open.

Robyn sprawled on the bed in nothing but a pair of leather knickers and a bondage harness. She snored faintly, eyes closed, dribbling a little. Nat stared for a moment, feeling the disappointment well up, but Robyn had looked tired, and now slept peacefully.

'Nat?' asked Rob, coming upstairs.

'Shush,' Nat answered, 'she's,' she broke off, Rob behind her.

Rob slipped an arm around her waist, dropping his other hand between her legs and stroking. 'Shall we go into the bathroom, have a shower and fuck?'

Nat shook her head. 'I'm going to go downstairs. I don't want to risk waking Robyn.' She smiled at Rob, leading him by the hand out of the bedroom. 'I'm going to put some cushions on the floor and stretch out, naked, where I can watch Mildred. We can't be too loud, but I want you inside me.'

--

'That's rather lovely.'

Nat looked up. She was sat in Rob's lap, Mildred in her arms. Mildred was wide awake but contentedly resting her head against Nat's chest. Rob's hand rested comfortably in her lap: they had made love slowly and Mildred had woken up for the last part, watching her quietly with big eyes.

Robyn came downstairs, grinning, in nothing but the leather knickers and harness. She knelt down next to them, leaning in, putting her arms around Rob's and her shoulders and kissing Nat.

Nat kissed Robyn eagerly. She thrust her tongue into Robyn's mouth and Robyn opened to her, her tongue exploring Nat's mouth.

After a few moments Robyn drew back, smiling, then leant in and kissed Rob.

Nat stroked Mildred tenderly, but Robyn's daughter seemed content being cuddled between them.

At last Robyn pulled back, grinning lustfully. Her breasts swung freely, rounded and plump, milk-heavy, just beginning to pull downwards.

'I hope the pair of you have not entertained yourselves too wildly.'

Nat shook her head, smiling shyly. 'Mildred woke up,' she shifted the silent baby tenderly, who turned to look at her, 'while we were making love. She didn't cry or anything.'

Robyn grinned. 'She watches a lot. She can probably smell the pheromones.' She sniggered. 'I can smell the pheromones. Nat in heat.'

Nat blushed. Rob leaned in and kissed her and she explored Rob's mouth with her tongue, all the while aware of Mildred in her arms, wanting to pull Rob closer, wanting to scratch his back, but scared to release Robyn's daughter.

As she broke the kiss with Rob, Robyn leant in and took Mildred from her.

'She's awake but not crying.' Robyn grinned. 'She wants entertainment.' She unzipped her knickers and drew them down, discarding them. She was neatly manicured and ripe, glistening with moisture.

Nat licked her lips. She could smell Robyn: milk and pleasure.

'We're going to put on a show for my daughter.' She wiggled her hips at Rob. 'You're going to eat this. Moist and self-lubricating.' She turned to Nat. 'While I eat your girl, Rob. She does have a lovely pussy.'

Nat blushed.

'She always tastes,' Robyn tilted her head. 'Mushrooms. Damp forests. Deliciously velvety and furry.'

Nat gulped as Robyn grabbed her and squeezed.

'Come on, Nat. Stretch out next to Mildred. Spread your legs. Rob, lie with your head near Nat's feet.'

Nat positioned herself, watching as Robyn settled herself first on Rob's face, wriggling and squirming. She was a little jealous: could see Robyn's enjoyment and hear her lover as he lapped at Robyn's pleasure.

'It'll take time, Nat,' Robyn said softly, looking at her.

Nat blushed, meeting her gaze. 'Oh.'

Robyn chuckled. 'Don't be jealous, Nat. There'll be time for us to do a lot of things.' Robyn lowered her head, licking.

Nat gasped in delight.

'But we'll start with this.'

Sunday 10th April

'Are you coming in for a tea break?'

Nat glanced at Alice. Alice wiped the sweat from her forehead. The white blouse she was wearing was smudged and dirty, stained with perspiration and the work they were doing in the Wolvercote Woods north of Oxford. The woods were a relatively new growth that had been let grow wild and now CVUK were being tasked to tidy it up, while still keeping it wild.

She wiped the perspiration from her own brow. 'We'll have a break here. It's too warm to move far unnecessarily.' She smiled at Tomas. 'Thanks for reminding us.'

Tomas nodded, half grinning and pointedly trying not to look too obviously at Alice. 'I'll – leave you to it then.'

Nat nodded and he sauntered off. Alice came over and sat down next to her. 'How's the job going?' Nat asked.

A smile flitted across Alice's face. 'It's too warm. This is nicer.' She smiled shyly. 'Tomas saw, didn't he?'

Nat nodded. 'Yes. But you've a right to dress and wear how and what you want.' She fetched over her bag and took out the packed lunch, sandwiches, a chocolate bar and a carton of squash. She wondered, briefly, what Rob and Robyn were doing, whether Robyn had taken Mildred home or the two of them –

Alice smiled shyly. 'I never thought I'd actually leave my room,' she looked around, lowering her voice, 'braless.'

Nat smiled encouragingly. 'You've got a slip on.'

Alice peeled the blouse from her skin. 'I walked to the bus with my bag across my chest. I didn't want anyone to see. I thought they'd laugh.'

Nat frowned. 'Alice, you're an attractive young lady. You're getting married in a few months. You've got a job, hobbies, friends. Why would anyone laugh at you?'

Alice looked up at her, wide eyed. 'Because —' she hesitated. 'Because I'm different. When we did,' she lowered her voice again, 'sex education,' she blushed, 'at school, they always told me it didn't apply to me. That no one would want to,' she coloured.

'Make love to you,' Nat finished.

Alice blushed. Nodded. 'It's not true though. Boys see,' she pulled her shoulders back awkwardly.

Nat nodded. 'They do. Some girls do as well.' She smiled. 'How is Howard?'

Alice blushed; nodded. 'He's lovely. I went round his house yesterday; his parents were away for the weekend.'

'Was it good?'

Alice nodded happily. 'We sat in the back garden and I let him take my blouse off.'

Nat smiled, remembering being sat in her own garden with Rob.

'We kissed a lot. He put my hand – between his legs. Inside his trousers.'

She finished off the sandwich. 'Did you enjoy – touching him?'

Alice nodded. 'I don't know where we're going to live when we're married. But it was nice, kissing Howard, while I had my hand there and he had his hands on my breasts.' She blushed. 'My hand got sticky.'

Nat laughed softly. 'Boys do, when they're excited.'

Nat took a mouthful of the juice.

'Does it – hurt?' Alice asked softly.

'What?'

'The first time,' Alice blushed. 'When a boy,' she trailed off.

'When you let a boy – come inside you.'

Alice blushed furiously, looking around. Nodded. 'Yes,' she whispered.

The first time with Gerald – had been her first time for that. Clovis had never penetrated her in any way, though he'd had her naked often enough.

'It can be,' she admitted. 'But Howard loves you. You love him. The first time, on your wedding night,' she paused. 'It may be awkward and clumsy; even painful. But remember you love him and he loves you. It takes time to discover – what – your partner likes.'

'What do you like? What does Rob like?'

Nat smiled. 'I like being sat in Rob's lap. He's quite tall. It's comforting, to have him wrap his arms around me. To burrow into his embrace.'

'Naked?'

Nat nodded. 'I like being naked around Rob,' she admitted, a little shyly. I just hope Robyn's not too comfortable being naked around him.

'What does Rob like?'

Big breasted airheads, according to Lucie. She shook her head, distracting the thought. 'He likes it when I'm indolent.'

'Indolent?'

Nat nodded. 'During long summer evenings we often stretch out on the bed, with the curtains open so the sun is streaming in. I lie in his arms and laze. He gradually pushes my top down and pulls my skirt up until, if anyone looked in the window,' she smiled at Alice.

'Until you'd be naked?'

Nat nodded, finishing off the drink and wiping her brow. 'It's nice, lying there, fully exposed but safe, in the arms of someone you love.'

Alice smiled. 'That sounds nice. I'd like to do that with Howard.'

--

'I hope you don't mind, I came straight from my conservation work –'

Douglas swept her into his embrace and hugged her tightly. 'Oh, Natalayiana, why would I object?' He kissed her cheek. 'You do so much. Is everything all right at home?'

She nodded. 'Yes,' she smiled broadly. 'We're – Rob and I – looking after a friend in our house so we're trying not to crowd her by always being there.'

Douglas nodded, offering Nat his arm. She slipped her arm through his.

'Thank you – for coming to see Vic off. I know he would have liked that you were there.'

Nat smiled. 'I liked him. He couldn't say much, the last few times I went to see him,' she trailed off.

Douglas smiled. 'He really appreciated you going round to see him. Even when he was too unwell to eat the Battenburg or drink the tea, he liked that you came round, that you kept that tradition you'd started going.'

Nat blushed a little. 'It was – he was a nice person. I wish,' she hesitated.

'Wishes don't achieve anything, Nat,' Douglas said softly, pushing open the front door of the house and holding it open for her.

It was cool inside. Cool, and somewhat emptier.

'Vic – Vic was – I suppose – my last tie to – other times,' Douglas explained. 'With him no longer here, it's time to think of the future.' He grinned at her. 'Giving you financial control over Clovis is the start of that.'

'He still gets – a stipend?'

Lord Merryweather nodded. 'A small amount a month. Not enough to do anything extravagant or wasteful with, but enough for food and bills and sundries. The rest,' he chuckled. 'The rest you control.'

'And his – mistress?'

Lord Merryweather smiled. 'I understand you denied Clovis Felicita this week?'

Nat nodded. 'He – spent time with her – after. At the funeral. I can see he's trying, but –'

Douglas held his hands up to stop her. 'Nat, Nat, Nat. Those actions are yours. I fully support you in them. You do not need to explain to me.' He smiled. 'I actually had a talk with Clovis, after you'd gone. I think,' he smiled, grinning at her. 'I think he even understood some of what I was saying.'

Nat blushed a little. 'I'm glad.'

'Come,' Douglas took her arm, 'there's someone I'd like you to meet. And a question I've got to ask you.'

'Oh?'

He led the way into the study. The walls were full of images of crows and ravens, pencil sketches and line drawings.

'I forget you change the pictures in here – weekly?'

Douglas grinned. 'Yes. If you study the pictures, look at their positioning. You'll see – over time – that it's the same places that I hang the pictures. But the pictures change.'

Nat looked around slowly, aware a slightly familiar person was sitting at the table.

Finally, she looked to them; frowned. Tried to remember where she'd seen them before.

'Barnet,' Douglas laughed, gesturing to a chair at the desk. Two cut glass tumblers with a thin line of whiskey stood waiting for them. 'Councillor Barnet.'

Councillor Barnet half stood, raising his own tumbler to her. 'Miss Harewood.'

Nat nodded. 'Uriah, is it?'

He chuckled. 'You are not quite the nervous, shy person you were, when Douglas first brought you into his study.'

Nat blushed. 'Thank you. Douglas – Lord Merryweather – is giving me many opportunities.'

Douglas sat, raising the glass and sniffing it but not raising it to his lips. 'Natalayiana.' He smiled. 'Oh, do not worry. It is nothing – bad or distasteful I need to ask you.'

Nat nodded. 'Of course. Ask away.'

Douglas nodded, taking a sip of his whiskey and not looking at her. He swirled the remnants in the glass. 'Are you a Were, Natalayiana Harewood?' he raised his gaze to hers as he spoke.

Nat blanched. Stared. Was intimately aware of the sweat on her skin. The thick, clammy dampness between her thighs. The soreness of her hands from using the lopper and the shears earlier. The smudges of earth and tree still on her cheeks.

A memory – from yesterday – of standing before Rob and Robyn. The pair of them sucking her nipples. Their fingers inside her kitty and her arse. Holding their heads to her chest while she climaxed. Biting. Licking. Nibbling.

'You're a dirty, abhorrent thing.' Her mother screaming, hurling video after video at her as she tried to flee the sitting room.

Her father spitting in her face.

Nat shuddered, trying to compose herself hurriedly. How long has passed? Is it obvious?

'N, n, no,' she stammered, looking at the floor, unable to look at either of them.

Douglas chuckled lightly. 'I only ask, Nat – and it would make no odds to me if you were – because your heart is so big. You work in social care. You work with a conservation charity in your own time. You look after a friend of yours.'

'No, no,' she managed to repeat, licking her lips to try and ease the dryness in her mouth. 'Looking after Robyn – and Mildred – '

'I know,' Douglas spoke softly, 'Dr Gold is interested in your friend's daughter.'

Nat felt the void yawning open beneath her once more. Could feel the emptiness freezing the sweat on her skin. Could almost feel her thatch turning to ice and her legs shivered from the cold.

'Dr Gold,' Douglas continued, unaware of her fear. 'Is someone to be very wary of. I would not like to think of you entrapped in her webs, Nat. She tends to get what she wants, one way or another.'

Nat blushed. The void had Dr Gold's face. Her voice. Her tongue. She was sinking into the void. Dr Gold's tongue was lapping at her thighs.

'Natalayiana.' Kelly swept her into her embrace, kissing her cheeks. 'My little Were daughter.' Her step-mother beamed with happiness. 'Life is shit, Natalayiana, but I will stand between you and as much of it as I can, until you are old enough to stand on your own. I don't know much about being Were, Nat, but you are my daughter and I am your mother and I love you.'

Nat fought to keep the tears from overwhelming her.

'Natalayiana,' Dr Gold purred. 'I am going to eat you up.'

Nat wiped the tears from her eyes. 'I know Dr Gold is,' she trailed off.

Lord Merryweather nodded, not having seemed to notice her – absence. 'Vic was involved with her laboratory, in some way. I could never persuade him against her, though he knew she was dangerous.'

'Everything she does,' said Uriah, 'is fully complicit. I've had her checked – discretely – a couple of times. Everything's above the board. Legal.'

Douglas snorted. 'Legal doesn't make it,' he shrugged. 'Legal is not necessarily good.'

'Why,' Nat asked –

'Because you are a tasty morsel,' Dr Gold answered, 'and I am going to feast on our body and turn you inside out.'

'Why,' she repeated, shaking her head, 'why did you ask me about – being a Were?'

Douglas shook his head. 'It was just a notion I had. A silly notion. You have such a big heart, Nat, and you ask for nothing for yourself.'

'You were adopted, weren't you?' said Uriah.

Nat stared at the councillor for a moment before nodding. 'Yes. My parents killed themselves.'

Uriah bowed his head. 'I am sorry. That must have been horrific.'

'You're horrific.' Her father spat in her face. Slapped her across the face so hard she staggered sideways into a chest of drawers. She collapsed, crying, and the chest wobbled.

'We should have drowned it at birth,' her mother screamed, pulling at the chest of drawers.

The chest toppled over, falling onto her, and she screamed in pain.

'Oh, Nat, Nat, Nat,' arms encircled her and held her. 'I am so sorry, Nat. This is too much for you.'

Nat looked up through the tears streaming down her face. Douglas held her, supporting her.

'I am sorry, Nat. Your parents were – terrible people?'

Nat gulped. Nodded.

Douglas held her, an arm around her waist, the other around her shoulders. 'I am sorry that that was brought up, Nat. I did not want to remind you of – old scars.'

Nat shook her head. She could smell stale cigarettes on Douglas' breath but otherwise he was a very comforting figure.

'My little flower-daughter.' Douglas' lips brushed her forehead with a kiss. 'I wish you had been my daughter, rather than Clovis.'

Nat wiped the tears from her eyes; Douglas released her, though she didn't step back from his nearness.

'I don't think Clovis would have made a good daughter. Though he will make a good son.'

Douglas pulled a face. 'My son went out with a beautiful, intelligent, caring, young woman, and forced her to kneel in front of him instead of making love to her.'

Nat blushed. 'My – former – relationship with your son –'

'I know, I know,' said Douglas, slightly irascibly, 'I don't want to know what my son did to you. I'm grateful you didn't run away that very first time when you saw him, when you realised he was my son.'

'I was so nervous that night. And you tricked me.' She smiled shyly. 'You let me think you were the chauffeur.'

Douglas drew her into his embrace once more and kissed her forehead. 'It is a trick I play on many. I do not think I have ever told you Nat, more so now than ever before, how much I appreciate your friendship.'

Nat blushed awkwardly, uncertain what to say.

Uriah laughed. 'Come on Douglas, you're embarrassing the girl. Nat, take a seat.'

Nat took her seat, taking a steadying sip of the whiskey.

'Cards?' Douglas suggested.

--

Nat pushed the door to the living room open and stared. Robyn sprawled, near-naked, on the sofa, in Rob's lap. She could see Rob was naked; Robyn was wearing black stockings and a suspender belt and nothing else. Rob's hands cupped her breasts, almost lifting them as offerings to her.

The room smelt of their pleasure.

'Nat!' Robyn purred. 'Come over here and feast.'

'I – didn't know you were staying.'

Robyn grinned, wriggling against Rob. 'I missed so much time yesterday, I thought I'd make up for it.'

'But I was out.'

Robyn nodded. 'You were missed. Join us.'

'Rob?'

He smiled blandly. 'Nat. We've been waiting for you. Yes, I'm naked, yes, I'm hard, rammed against Robyn's cheeks. But we've not fucked.'

Nat raised an eyebrow. 'I can smell you.'

Robyn smiled. 'I didn't say I hadn't come. Three times from the feel of your boyfriend's cock, and his hands on my boobs. And yes, Rob came over my arse after I came the second time. But we showered separately and we've not kissed. Nat,' she begged, sitting up, pushing Rob's hands away. 'If you want me to go, I will.' She sighed. 'But I want to make love to you while your boyfriend cuddles me. I want to kneel before you and eat you. Rob wants to kneel before you and eat you.'

Robyn stood up, Rob a moment later. He was as hard as she'd ever seen him.

She shook her head. 'I'm tired. I'm stressed. I'm sweaty. I'm not –'

'That's the you that I want,' said Rob, taking her hand. 'What can I do to take your stress away?'

Nat looked at him. At his length. Shook her head. 'That's more of you than I can take at any time.' She sighed. 'I need to pee. Don't go anywhere, don't do anything.'

She headed upstairs, shut the bathroom door behind her. Why did Lord Merryweather ask me about whether I was a Were? It was – I hadn't expected it. Not from him. She shuddered. Undressed and sat on the loo.

'I love Robyn,' she said softly. 'I love Rob. There is no way I can take Rob when he's that big. Not in human form.' She scowled. Sighed. 'I will have to tell Robyn at some point – soon – that I'm a Were.' She sighed again. 'She hates them. She'll hate me for being one, and for not telling her.'

When she was finished she cleaned herself with a flannel. I'm about to help my boyfriend fuck my best friend. She smiled sadly. What did they do when I wasn't here? Did they really just cuddle and talk? If that was all they did, how did they resist going further? If they'd gone further and told me –

She opened the bathroom door and padded downstairs. Rob was leaning against the mantle, his back to the room. Robyn was rocking her daughter's cradle: Mildred seemed to be sleeping comfortably. Both looked up as she descended.

'Rob, I want to watch you kissing Robyn. She's a beautiful, shapely, woman. Enjoy holding and cuddling her.'

Rob grinned, taking Robyn in his arms. They kissed: she wrapped her arms tight around him; deliberately pressing and rubbing her chest again him; he grabbed her arse tight.

Nat watched, smiling faintly. They looked like they belonged together. Both were taller than her but there was less height difference between them than her and Rob.

You put them together. Lucie did say you weren't Rob's type.

You love Rob. You love Robyn. You trust them.

She stared at them. They were still kissing, but Rob was fondling and squeezing Robyn's boob and she was fumbling at his waist –

'That's enough,' she snapped and, almost unbelievably, they pulled apart.

Nat smiled. 'I have an idea.' She blushed, a little. 'Something I'd like to try.'

Monday 11th April

Nat smiled in relief as she opened the door and saw Marianne. There were fresh flowers on the reception desk and the air smelled of violets, one of Marianne's favourite smells.

'Marianne. How was the holiday?'

The receptionist looked up and smiled broadly. 'Nat. You look – happy.' She came out from behind the counter and hugged Nat tightly. 'And when I say happy,' she took Nat's hands and drew back, looking her up and down before drawing her close again. 'I mean you've been very well taken care of.'

Nat blushed.

Marianne chuckled. 'Has the dashing Rob been seeing to – every part of you?'

She'd knelt before Robyn last night, barely needing to touch her before the other woman had climaxed. After that she'd drawn Robyn down and the two of them had made love, tongues down each other's throats and hands between each other's hips. They'd shared pleasure and then she'd beckoned Rob down and he'd taken Robyn from behind, each thrust of his hips eliciting a more and more excited cry from Robyn, each thrust sending ripples of pleasure into her.

'I can see he did,' Marianne smirked, giggling, holding her hand over her mouth.

'And you?' Nat blushed. 'How did it go – with Albert?'

A big smile crossed Marianne's face. 'This old girl's still got it.' She beamed. 'I booked us a couple of nights away, the Peak District. A couple of rooms, made it clear nothing was – certain.'

Nat nodded. Lying underneath Robyn, holding her, feeling her pleasure as Rob took her, as Rob filled her. And then afterwards –

'The weather was lovely. We went for a walk in the peaks. There wasn't anyone around. We held hands. We kissed.' A touch of colour touched Marianne's cheeks. 'In Miller's Dale Albert felt me up.'

Nat blushed.

'I know it's not much for you young ones. But I'm over sixty. I've been without anyone for,' she shook her head. 'We had a nice meal in the evening. I invited him back to my room for a nightcap.'

Nat grinned. Afterwards – they'd lain in a large bundle for a long while, sharing aftershocks and lazy kisses. Then Rob had pulled out of Robyn and Robyn had rolled, taking her with her, so that Nat lay in Robyn's arms. They'd kissed for a while, warming each other up gradually, then –

'We kissed.' Marianne almost blushed. 'We made love. In the morning,' her eyes twinkled, 'we made love again.'

'I'm pleased for you. Was the second day as good?'

Marianne nodded. 'We went for an even longer walk. It was –'

The inner door opened and Bryan stuck his head round. 'Nat, I've got someone for you to see.'

--

Nat stared for a moment. 'Jack? I mean, Mr Mathers. What can I do for you?'

Jack smiled blandly, thanking Bryan as he withdrew.

'You didn't want – Bryan in here as well?'

Jack shook his head. 'No. I've spoken to him as well. You know I work for Homes for Weres.'

Nat nodded, taking a seat. 'I do. They've never –'

'They would like to meet you. Apologise, I believe.'

Nat raised an eyebrow. 'Really? Now? Why?'

Jack smiled, seeming to hesitate for a moment. 'I'm – not altogether sure why. They have changed their plans, no more homes or game shows or anything like that.' He hesitated again. 'They have not shared their intentions with me, just that a couple of the high level managers are coming over next week, and one of the things they would like to do is meet you.'

Nat frowned. 'And your thoughts on it?'

Jack smiled. 'I am naturally wary. As you should be. I *do* believe they are trying, but – believe me, I have told them nothing of what I know – but why now and why you, I do not know.'

'Did you know about the camera feeds from their – property?'

'The property where you were –' Jack shook his head. 'No.'

'Where Rob was shot, Gerald was abused and I was stripped naked and forced to admit, on video, that I was a Were.'

Jack nodded. 'No, I did not know. I think I joined – after.'

'Why?' Nat sat forward. 'What made you join *them*? And what did you tell Bryan?'

'They offered me money, Nat.' Jack sat back. 'No office work, I can work from home, I'm not dependent on any council –'

'No, you're dependent on H4W –'

'As you're dependent on SHiP –'

Nat looked away, trying to hide her scowl.

'If you wanted, Nat, I think you could join them. As an ambassador. You wouldn't need to reveal you're a Were –'

'I'm not,' Nat protested.

Jack laughed softly. 'No? You are looking younger, Nat. Not so stressed. Your hair is getting subtly redder. I can smell the forest, the undergrowth, on you. It's not parched anymore.' He grinned. 'You're changing.'

Nat looked away.

'Nat, I will always keep your secret. But on the off-chance this may be the real thing –'

'Real thing?' Nat snorted. 'Thank you, Jack. But no thank you. I don't trust H4W.'

--

'When's the convention?' Jezabel asked, for not the first time.

Nat smiled, passing her the mug of warm orange juice. Jezabel had let her go into the kitchen for the first time. It was small, superficially clean and tidy, but there was dust in the corners and Nat had seen a few spots of mould.

'Three and a half week's time.' She took a seat. 'Rob will take you and I there on the Friday. We've only one room, I'm afraid, so we'll have to share the bed or if there's a sofa I'll take that.'

Jezabel nodded. 'Is it the whole hotel?'

Nat nodded. 'They're using the facilities of the hotel. There's discussions, games – board, and other kinds, costume competitions, book readings, a few films, well known and experimental, art house, and,' she shrugged. 'I don't know what else. I know one of the organisers, that's how I got free tickets.'

'And you never know,' Jezabel smiled knowingly.

Nat smiled. 'You might meet someone. If you do, and I'm not there, leave something on the doorhandle. I'll find – somewhere else – so you've some privacy.'

Jezabel nodded her thanks. 'I'm not – it's a big thing but not. To just know that someone – anyone – is happy to –'

'Spend time with you?'

'Fuck me,' Jezabel answered, almost bitterly. 'You're very kind, Nat, I couldn't have got this far without you. And I couldn't possibly – *go out* – with anyone. But going out – and for two and a half days,' she shook her head in amazement. 'I'm scared and delighted and terrified and looking forwards to it.' She took a mouthful of her drink. 'But I still want to get – something – there. Even if it's just felt up with my huge fake squirrel boobs.'

Nat forced herself to smile. 'You don't have to –'

'I do,' Jezabel insisted. 'When I know, when someone's,' she trailed off.

'You're putting a lot of pressure onto yourself, Jezabel.'

Jezabel grimaced. 'If I didn't think there was a chance of getting anything, why would I go?'

Tuesday 12th April

Nat knocked on the side door of the 'Hale and well met' pub and stepped back. After a moment there was a call from within; the sounds of movement.

The pub was situated on the outskirts of North Oxford, in a back street. It looked more like a corner house than a dedicated pub, with a small frontage and no parking. The sign creaked in the slight wind, a faded hand raised in greeting, surrounded by a still-bright green wreath.

The door was yanked open and Nat looked up into the eyes of a tall, curly-haired man, with a layered green and black beard.

'You're from SHiP?' he spoke surprisingly softly.

Nat nodded, offering her badge. He waved his hand dismissively.

'Come in, come in.' He went to take her hand then rolled his eyes and stepped back. 'Follow me through. Shut the door behind you. My daughter's in the main bar.'

The bar was small; homely. Nat doubted more than twenty people could fit in at once. Internally, it looked like a cross between a house and a pub, as if somehow it had been changing from one to the other and got stuck mid-change. Most of the lights were off, only a couple over the bar on, and barely any light got through the small windows.

'The file said,' she began.

The publican nodded. 'Aye. Call me James, by the way. This is Petra.'

His daughter sat on a bar stool. Short brown hair and a pair of sunglasses; a shirt and cardigan; long skirt.

'Forgive me if I don't get up,' she smiled in Nat's direction.

Nat nodded. 'Of course.'

'It's this, you see,' James leaned on the bar, smiling at his daughter. 'Petra's off to university in a few months. Over the last — six months or so — she's been losing her sight.'

'The government should —'

He snorted. 'They *should*, but they haven't. Even with medical evidence, they've rejected our claims. They say she's young, she has partial sight, she doesn't need anything.'

Petra smiled blandly.

'How much — can you see, Petra? May I call you Petra?'

Petra lowered her gaze. Nat realised it was so she could look over her glasses.

'I can hardly see you in the dark. You must be short.' She smiled. 'Or my direction is off and you can throw your voice well.'

Nat shook her head. Realised that Petra probably couldn't see that. 'No, I'm not a ventriloquist.'

James nodded. 'Think about it. Petra will need to get between classes. Up and down stairs, or a lift. Her own room or sharing with someone.' He shook his head. 'It'd be different if it was her second year and she knew the site.'

'At the moment, I can just see – impressions. Shapes. Outlines. Blurs. The doctors don't know why.' Petra sighed.

'And you put all this on the form?'

James nodded. 'Aye. Medical certificates and notes from two different doctors. No benefits, they said.'

Nat nodded. 'I would like to go through the form with you, Mr Parsons, and ask some questions of Petra. Which would you prefer I did first?'

--

'Door's open, Nat,' Robyn called as Nat raised her hand to rap on the glass.

Nat pushed the door open, closed it behind her and went through to the sitting room. Sunlight streamed in through the window: the flat was at the top of a steep garden. Entrance to the other flat was around the back, and no one had any cause to come up to the door except to see Robyn.

Robyn was wearing a long cardigan, held together with a single button, which didn't cover much. She looked refreshed and awake.

'Just had a long sleep,' she smiled. 'Mildred will still be asleep for a few hours.' She grinned, unbuttoning the cardigan. 'Fancy sunbathing?'

Nat blushed. Nodded shyly. 'I might start – on my front.'

Robyn laid the cardigan out and put a cushion at the end furthest from the window; put another cushion down next to it.

'I enjoyed the weekend.' She drew Nat into her embrace and kissed her.

After a few moments they drew apart.

'So did I,' Nat smiled.

'I didn't mean – just the sex,' Robyn said. 'It was nice – having company. Bodies to hold and be held by.'

Nat removed her blouse and laid it over the end of the sofa.

'Why are you wearing a slip, Nat?' Robyn asked, unbuttoning her trousers and tugging them down.

Nat stepped out of her trousers and peeled the slip off. She shook her head. 'There's a new member of staff. He objected to me being braless.'

Robyn snorted, laying her hand over Nat's heart. 'None of his business.'

Nat nodded. 'Bryan's – appeasing him, I think.' She tugged her knickers down and laid them on top of her blouse.

Robyn put a hand on her hip and knelt down.

'We're not – we shouldn't –'

Robyn looked up at her and chuckled. 'I noticed the other day your fur was coming through red again.' She stroked the soft fur gently. 'At uni, you did have a glorious blaze of red fur, Nat.' She caressed Nat's thighs. 'Does Rob like your hairy legs?'

Nat nodded. 'He calls me – his little animal.'

Robyn nodded, still stroking her legs and thighs. 'If I was Rob, I'd spend hours just caressing your legs and eating your pussy.'

Nat blushed a little. 'We are – quite physical.'

Robyn grinned, lying down. 'Tell me about it. I've had and been had by your Rob, remember.' She took Nat's hand and squeezed it. 'I always knew you had hidden depths.' She sniggered. 'To accommodate Rob, you'd need them.'

Nat lay down, face down, re-arranging the pillow.

'Are you and Rob – okay – with what we did?'

Nat nodded slowly. 'It was – a big step. We both enjoyed it, individually and collectively –'

'You need to make sure you talk to Rob, Nat. The man absolutely adores you.'

Nat pulled a face. 'He seemed to enjoy – having you in his lap.'

'Don't get me wrong,' Robyn rolled onto her side, stroking Nat's back gently, 'we both enjoyed it. And I enjoyed you and Rob. It was lovely making love to you and then having Rob join in.' She trailed her fingers over Nat's rump. We didn't fuck while you were out, Nat.'

'I know,' Nat half protested.

'I don't think you do,' Robyn said softly. 'As much as I enjoyed having Rob front and back, he's the boyfriend of my best friend. I'm not going to sacrifice you for a quick shag, Nat. I know – with Gerald, we did things. But Rob's good for you.'

Nat nodded. She went to stretch her hand out for a very plump and inviting breast, but hesitated, drew her hand back.

'I'm not going to come round this week, Nat.' Robyn continued caressing her back gently. 'I want to make sure you and Rob are okay.'

'You can,' Nat protested, 'we will be okay.'

'I'm not saying you won't,' Robyn smiled, 'but that was a treat, for all of us. I'm on my own, and you need to be okay with Rob and Rob needs to be okay with you.'

Nat nodded. 'We are. I think we are.'

'I hope so.' Robyn leant over and kissed her shoulder. 'I owe you so much, Nat. And Rob for allow – supporting you in it.'

Nat blushed. 'That's – what is still a little between us, I think. Rob kind of wishes he'd been there, if only to see – what was done.'

Robyn nodded. 'Rob's – very supporting, Nat. Take him away at the weekend. Give him a filthy time. I can loan you whatever you want – I've got loads of bondage gear.'

Nat blushed. The thought of – changing for Rob. Bringing him to heights to make him change. That could be – she thought deliciously. I do want to spend time with his Were, properly.

She sighed to herself. I want to have his Were – snuffling my belly. Between my legs. I want his Were to smell my pleasure.

'I think, when I come round next week,' Robyn smiled, 'I'm not going to stop offering you milk, but I'll decant it first.'

'It's okay, Rob won't –'

'Rob was embarrassed, Nat. Even after we'd had our fun. I'm sure he wouldn't object, but I'd rather not – cause anything to come between the pair of you.'

Nat nodded reluctantly. As much as she wanted to do filthy things with Rob – 'can I tell you something, Robyn?' she asked, sitting up.

Robyn rolled onto her back. 'Of course you can.'

'Being – fed by you,' she blushed a little, 'the first few seconds – are a turn on. I've – enjoyed your body often enough,' she rushed on, colouring slightly. 'But when you wrap your arm round me and I'm suckling, drinking milk,' she blushed furiously, 'it's – maternal.'

Robyn almost sobbed. 'Nat. I'll decant at your house but you need to come here. I'll always feed you.' She held out her arms invitingly.

'No, I meant –' Nat paused.

Robyn lay back down on the floor, stretched out, arms still inviting. 'Come on, Nat.'

Nat clambered over and lay down on top of her, arranging herself into position. She latched on and Robyn's arm went round her shoulders.

'I know your mother was a bitch,' Robyn said softly, 'but Kelly was a lovely person.'

Nat suckled and drank greedily, trying not to think of anything. She was a baby and her mother loved her, her mother would protect her, care for her, support her. She sucked harder, her mother stroking her hair and cuddling her.

At last she sat up, licking her lips. It wasn't her mother, or Kelly, but Robyn, smiling indolently at her.

'You were certainly a thirsty girl.' She smiled. 'You can go back to sunbathing if you want, in which case it's probably time you laid on your back and let the sun warm you between your legs.' Her grin broadened. 'Or you can nuzzle up to mama, lay your head on my bosom and have a rest.'

Nat shifted over slightly, resting her head against the warm slopes of Robyn's bosom.

Robyn was just so warm and cuddly. Safe, she realised. Robyn loved her and Rob, would never come between them. And if she couldn't have sex with Robyn, cuddling with her was almost as good.

'You've been so strong for so long, Nat. That thing – when you were kidnapped. Work. What Gerald did.'

She could feel Robyn gently stroking her.

'I need to get a comb so I can comb your hair when you're like this.'

Nat murmured contentedly. 'Kelly never combed my hair, it always used to tangle. But she used to pamper me when –' she bit off hurriedly – when I changed back from being a Were.

'Time of the month?'

Nat nodded. As a teenager, hit by puberty and periods and Weredom, it had been hellish – at least until her parents were gone and Kelly adopted her. For the first year or two after Kelly adopted her, after each change, Kelly would share a bath with her. Her step-mother would clean her up and hold her and Nat would cry and curse and bewail her fate.

Kelly always said it was a blessing. That I was human and animal. That I was more than human.

After the bath – or as she grew older and more experienced in coping with it, the shower – she'd dress in pyjamas and a dressing gown and share Kelly's bed and they'd talk about boys and eat ice cream.

By the time she was of an age to go to university, she knew how to control her emotions, how to stop having to change. With that maturity, and moving away to university –

Nat burst into tears, burying her face between Robyn's breasts.

Robyn rocked her gently, arm around her shoulder, other hand stroking her hair, shushing her softly. 'It's okay, Nat. It's okay. I'm not going anywhere.'

'It's scary,' she murmured, lifting a hand and stroking a warm curve.

'What's scary, Nat?' Robyn asked softly.

Nat raised her head. 'My parents were evil. Nasty. They're gone, thankfully. Kelly was much nicer, a proper mother. She's gone,' she rushed on, 'Gerald was nice and we're not together anymore. I've Rob, but,' she sighed.

Robyn wrapped both her arms around her and drew her up. 'Gerald wasn't that nice, Nat. He made you afraid. He didn't talk, didn't open up.' She leant in and kissed Nat. 'Rob is far better for you. Next time,' her eyes twinkled, 'if there is a next time, it would be lovely to be in this position, with you on top, and then have Rob join us.' She smiled lasciviously. 'I want to watch Rob taking and bringing you.'

Nat blushed. 'I'm lucky, aren't I? He really cares for me.'

Robyn nodded. 'He does. Even if I wanted to steal him from you, I'm not sure I could.'

Nat frowned.

'The Sunday morning, when you were out. I was lying in Rob's lap. Both of us naked, I'll admit. He was talking about you. Called you his little squirrel girl. He loves you, Nat. He lusts after you. He,' she hesitated.

'He what?'

'He said something – he probably shouldn't have. But don't take it the wrong way. We were – sharing.'

'What? What did Rob say?'

'He said,' Robyn smiled. 'He said, for all the women he's had, for all the things he's done with them, the best is,' she hesitated again, almost leering.

'What?' Nat asked, frustrated and scared.

'Rob said the best thing he's ever done is kneel before you. He likes eating you, Nat. He loves the taste of you in his mouth. It brings him pleasure, bringing you that way.'

Nat blushed.

'He loves your hairiness. Don't ever shave,' she chuckled. 'He said he's done far more intimate and erotic things with you than with anyone else.'

Wednesday 13th April

'Why did you – ask me to come and see you?'

Dr Gold raised an eyebrow sardonically. She was dressed in a smart business suit, black blouse buttoned to the neck.

'I did not ask you to come and see me. I summoned you. There is a difference.'

'You cannot just –'

'I can,' Dr Gold answered flatly. 'Make no mistake, Miss Harewood. If you fail to obey me, your friend Robyn and her daughter, Mildred, will suffer.'

'You cannot – why do you – what do you want?'

'If I wanted,' she leaned back in her seat, 'I could order you to strip naked and summon the guard to give you a full body cavity search.'

Nat stared. 'Why? You wouldn't?'

Dr Gold chuckled. 'I enjoy humiliating you, Harewood. You are an interesting – pawn.'

'Pawn?'

She nodded. 'What is Lord Merryweather to you?'

Nat shook her head. 'A friend. Nothing more.'

Dr Gold chuckled. 'Is it true that the imbecilic Clovis used to wank over you?'

Nat stared. 'What? How –'

'It's called bukkake, Nat. You were such a little mouse at university.' She smirked. 'Rob is obviously putting a spine into you. Regularly.' She smiled. 'How did

141

Robyn take the fact her daughter is the daughter of a Were?'

Nat shook her head. 'She didn't like it, obviously. Why are you –'

'Nat.'

Her voice cracked out and Nat froze.

'You are a good bellringer, Nat. But I think you need to be reminded about discipline and obedience. Strip to the waist.'

Nat stared. 'No. You cannot make me. I'm here because you asked me to come, you sent a message to SHiP –'

'Yes, I did.' Dr Gold glowered. 'I believe SHiP is now partnered with Were Legal Opportunities.'

Nat stared. Blinked. 'What? Yes. How did you –'

'I sit on their board.'

Nat felt the ground yawning open beneath her feet. 'You – what? You instructed that – Thomas?'

The doctor waved her hand dismissively. 'I gave you an order, Nat. Obey it, or find yourself in trouble at work. Again. And I will punish Robyn for it as well. *That* should motivate you to be obedient.'

'You cannot harm Robyn. This is between you and I –'

She nodded. 'Yes. And yesterday I came to collect her – personally – and what did I find?'

Nat blanched.

'I found a certain office junior writhing naked in the arms of the mother of a daughter of a Were. Are you a Were-lover, Nat? I know Rob is a shape-shifter, and Robyn is not, but Weres – do tend to react to and attract other Weres.'

Nat shook her head desperately. 'Please, don't hurt Robyn.' I cannot – I must – I cannot – I do not want Rob to hear – from Dr Gold. *Nothing* happened with Robyn. 'Please,' she begged, fumbling at the buttons of her blouse.

'You took so long, the cost has increased.' Dr Gold spoke coldly. 'Strip naked.'

--

Nat froze. She could smell patchouli and wild garlic, and its earthiness called to her, tugged at her senses. For a moment she almost felt like she was in a dark forest, with rain dripping all around and tangled root systems underfoot. She breathed deeply and the sensations passed and she was back in the back stairs of the new age shop.

She continued up the stairs, not knowing what to expect. The paint was a faded green and peeling; a single lightbulb swung slowly high above. The shop had been an overwhelming experience of crystals that refracted light and drew her in and multiple conflicting overlapping scents, oils and essences and the tinkling of differently tuned windchimes.

The landing opened into a large room, used as a stockroom, and off it another room, with the door half closed and the room beyond in darkness, but from which she could hear lowered voices.

'Hello?' she asked, advancing.

The door opened fully and a woman came into view, a broad smile on her face.

'Hello. You must be Natalayiana. I am Raven.'

She wore a white halter neck dress which contrasted beautifully with her dark skin. Silver earrings glittered in her ears and she wore a necklace of small animal skulls and bones.

Nat nodded, uncertain, slightly overawed.

'Welcome, Natalayiana. Come into the doorway.'

The woman – Raven – took a half step back. Nat stepped into the doorway, peeking into the room beyond. Three people smiled or waved in greeting from a circle of about a dozen chairs. An old, threadbare carpet; a rainbow flag covered the window though light still shone through it. Several Himalayan salt lamps decorated the room and there was a selection of drums on a table against one wall.

'Everyone is blessed before they enter the circle; before they enter the room. It helps to leave behind anything negative. Incense or bells?'

Nat drew her attention back to Raven. 'Oh. I'd prefer bells.'

The woman drew a pair of Tibetan bells from the table and lifted them up in front of her. Nat stared guiltily for a moment. Ringing Laetitia's bell –

The bells chimed and she found herself in the room. She could smell the wild garlic strongly with the patchouli an undercurrent.

'Seven times, sister,' Raven smiled, 'one for each chakra.'

Nat couldn't help but smile. Raven's voice was like warm honey, or warm chocolate. Something to luxuriate in. Something to bask in.

'If it seems strange or awkward,' Raven spoke softer, just to her, 'do not worry about it. Let it be. These things take time.'

She struck the bells together for the seventh time and Nat felt her body tingling all over. It wasn't sexual and it wasn't Were – it was hard to describe. Like, for just an instant, she'd been born anew and caught naked in a summer thunderstorm and woken up with the light of the full moon blazing down at her.

She shivered and smiled.

Raven smiled. 'The first time you hear the bells tingle through you,' she grinned broadly, 'it's like watching your grandchild being born and the memory of your first time and innocence anew.'

She stepped back, returning the bells to the table. She picked up a small drum, which was patterned red and black; they could have been flashes of colour or even feathers, Nat wasn't sure.

'I think this will suit you, Natalayiana,' she smiled. 'Take a seat, and we will begin.'

Nat sat down. Nodded to the others; two older women, one younger man.

'Before we begin the drum circle, we call out to the four directions. Some call these the compass points or the cardinal points. We call to above, to below, and to within. This is so the Ehi, the guardian spirits, angels, the beings beyond humanity, know we are here and that this is an offering and to bless and support us.'

Nat followed what Raven was doing, as the others did. Raven spoke sometimes in a harsh, strident tone, as if intending to batter the doors to the other realms, and sometimes in a soft, crooning manner, as if enticing them to open. Always the sounds, the language, was musical and beautiful, though she had no idea what Raven was saying.

Raven smiled, her happiness illuminating the darkened room. 'The circle is open and a safe space. For those of you who have not drummed with me before,' and she flashed Nat and one of the older women a smile, 'we will drum to something specific. I will lead the rhythm and you will join in when ready. If your drum takes a different beat, that is not a problem. You will find the rhythms unite and splinter and do their own thing and then reunite again. Some call that drum singing.'

She smiled at all of them. 'There is no right or wrong to this. As we have two new people with us tonight, we will journey to what we individually think of as a safe space. It could be the wild open plains. It could be a deep forest. A deserted beach. Wherever you feel safe.'

Raven smiled, picking up her drum and running her fingers around the side of it. 'Close your eyes. When the beat begins, listen. When you are ready, add the voice of your drum. Start seeing your safe place. You may be there instantly, you may find you are walking towards it.' She chuckled. 'But also, if nothing comes to you, if you only hear the drums and do not see anything, do not feel anything, that is not wrong either. This is a journey,' and she lifted her beater.

Nat closed her eyes. Lucie had suggested she try shamanic drumming, amongst other things. Having seen a skull imprinted over Lucie's face had been a shocking thing, but Lucie had been more intrigued than alarmed. Rob had never heard anything like it, from any other Were.

The skull had been bad enough, that could just have been tiredness or a reaction to something. But to see a huge worm-like tongue and to see a skeletal hand claw her up – there is more to this –

The drum beat overwhelmed her, four solid, slow beats. She was surprised to realise she was already beating along, that the drum she'd been given had a high, strident, caw-like, sound.

Nat could smell the patchouli and found herself in a forest. Not a forest she could see, but the scents and sounds, the feel of it beneath her paws – paws! She flexed her feet and felt her toes move.

Not changed. Phew.

The drumbeat continued and she was back there in an instant.

Ancient oaks. *Not* oaks. Redwoods. Something massive. A primordial forest. A forest without a town, a world without civilisation, a world with trees. Trees so high and thickly flourishing that they blocked out the sun, though she could feel light and warmth upon her skin.

Rain. *Not* rain. A dampness to the air. Ancient forests, deep rivers, wide lakes. A world without humans.

Nat smiled. She could sense creatures in the forest, but they were so small – or so large – that neither were any threat to her or she to them.

Scattered rain washed over her. A rain of nuts and berries, leaves and twigs. She lifted her head and could see the tree advancing straight into the sky, except it wasn't a tree, it was a bridge, and she was scurrying along it, snout close to the ground.

The wood was slippery beneath her paws, beneath her claws, but there was no fear of falling. I am ācweorna she thought, scurrying along the wooden road from the planet to the sky.

She could feel the winds as she left the world behind and used her tail to balance herself, shifting this way and that to withstand the breezes. She gripped tightly for a moment, waiting for the squall to pass, and then continued scurrying upwards into the sky, except now it was a tree leading into a lunar landscape of huge white boulders. Between the boulders was squid-like inky blackness, but it was easy to jump, and almost fly, from boulder to boulder.

The rhythm changed, the world shifted, and she was clinging to a rock as it fell out of the sky. Slid down the tree bridge and then down the tree, landing on all fours, bracing herself with her tail, and then she could smell wild garlic and patchouli again, and her fingers were cramping and her hand was slowing, the beat disintegrating.

Nat looked up. Opened her eyes.

--

'What – how – did I see?'

Raven smiled broadly. 'What did you see?'

Nat blushed. The session had finished, the time had flown by, but the first – experience – had been the strongest and the strangest of all.

'I was in a forest. I couldn't see, but I just knew it was. There was a tree, I scampered up it,' she smiled awkwardly. 'It was a bridge into the sky, then – I don't know. The moon? Then the rhythm changed and I was coming back, riding one of the rocks, I think,' she shook her head incredulously.

Raven smiled, her look knowing. 'It is the beat of the drum. It changes cognition. Some people see things, like you have. Some experience nothing. Some get sounds, or scents,' she smiled, putting her hand on Nat's arm momentarily. 'It sounds like a very interesting journey.'

'What does it mean?'

Raven chuckled. 'It can mean anything. Or nothing. The drums speak to you. The woods – any woods – are often a safe place for people. The journey into the sky and then the moon.' She smiled broadly. 'I suggest you write down as much as you can remember. Will we see you again next month?'

Nat nodded. 'Oh, yes. Definitely.'

Thursday 14th April

George looked up at her and half scowled.

'Why is your hair loose?'

'I'm running late,' she tried not to scowl. 'I didn't have time to braid it or tie it up.'

George almost grinned. 'It's nice. Hadn't realised it fell to your hips.'

Nat nodded, going to grab the file for the next client she had to see. Marianne had said both Thomas and Bryan were out; a godsend, in some ways, but George –

She'd had strange dreams all night, though the morning had driven the memory of what they were from her. She could remember the forest, the bridge, the sky, the drumming, clearly, from last night's first drumming session. Could still feel the breeze and smell the rain.

I expected it to be – more incense. More – mystical. Maybe it's Raven's way. She almost smiled. I'm definitely going again.

'You could play Godiva, you know. With hair like that. You could get away with wearing nothing.'

Nat half heard, turning to scowl at George as she scooped up the file. 'What? Never mind, I'm late already.'

George was suddenly there, blocking her way. 'You're furry enough.'

Nat scowled. 'George. I've got a job to do. Three clients to visit.'

He moved towards her and she backed up, bumping into the desk.

'George,' she protested.

'You need to make it up to me,' he glared. 'I don't want much. Some recompense for what you've caused. No one else is in. We can use Bryan's office.'

Nat shook her head. 'No. No, George. You love Evie. You want to get back together with her. She wouldn't want you to do this. And my boyfriend really wouldn't like —'

'You wouldn't have to tell him,' George put his hands on her hips, pinning her to the desk. 'Come on, Nat. I've seen you naked. No one will know. Just let me —'

'I'm not Evie, George,' she hissed. 'If I raise my voice, Marianne will hear. If Marianne hears, there is no way back from this.'

He scowled at her furiously. Stared at her chest. 'Get. Out,' he growled, moving out of the way.

Nat fled.

--

Nat headed down the road, her mind awhirl. Marianne might have realised something was off, the fact she'd left without waiting for her to reappear. George — she shuddered. I have to put a complaint in about him.

I don't want to.

I have to.

She shook her head, realising she was nearing her new client's house. It was brightening up, the sun peeking through the April clouds, but it was still Blackbird Leys. Nat sighed. The government said the area wasn't as bad as it used to be, but that wasn't saying much.

There was still car crime, road-racing, theft, robbery, burglary, drug dealing and more. A few of their clients had ended up in Blackbird Leys. It was a difficult place to get out of, under any circumstances.

She turned the corner, following the edge of a park, dimly aware of a couple of people ahead of her on the pavement. She hurried on, hoping she'd get another chance to have a look at the file she'd brought out with her. She'd read it yesterday, but in between Dr Gold and the shamanic drumming, all memory of it had been driven out of her head.

Wolf whistles made her look up, in surprise. No one wolf –

A group of youths blocked the pavement, some of them probably no more than fifteen, though one looked noticeably older.

'Woah, what we got here then?'

'Bring it on, skinny.'

'We can show you a good time, love.'

She shook her head, veering off the pavement and into the road to get past them.

'Hey, don't be like that!'

'Hey, bitch!'

A hand pulled at her sleeve and she looked up, stepping away simultaneously.

Two lunged at her and a fist caught her in the side. She gasped in surprise, dropping the file.

A car swerved by, sounding its horn.

Another fist hit her in the side. Hands groped at her chest, at her thighs. Someone kicked her knee out and she went down hard, crying out as she hit the concrete and asphalt.

There was laughter. A few more kicks. She huddled in on herself, trying to wrap into a ball.

A hand in her hair, pulling her head up. Then she was slammed back down again.

Awareness.

Consciousness.

Pressure.

No light penetrated the inky blackness. There was just the liquid darkness. A darkness that moved, that breathed, that oozed.

The liquid lapped against something unexpected. Something that was not of the deep.

Slapped and murmured.

Susurrated.

The echoes, the ripples, rebounded.

The ocean breathed.

The water breathed.

The consciousness breathed.

There was water – inside – beyond – the barrier. It found the borders quickly.

A box.

Airtight. Sealed. Containing water, like and unlike itself.

Buried in the deep of the ocean.

Deep enough for the glass box to be crushed open by the pressure of the water, but it was not.

Time passed.

Aeons passed.

The ocean could wait.

The ocean was limitless.

Part 3

Friday 6th May

Nat sat up, gasping, struggling to breathe, convinced she was drowning, that her lungs were full of water, that she was deep undersea and bring crushed by the pressure.

Am I the ocean or am I the box?

She screamed, shuddering. Everything was too bright, too light, too fresh. She flung herself round, diving down deep beneath the pillows and the quilt.

Heard voices. Were the voices from the box or were they hers?

A hand on her arm.

If I am the ocean, this body is too small to contain it. She shuddered. Wriggled.

Voices, going away.

After a while, she felt movement. Turned her head.

A wrinkled, mostly scrunched up face looked at her. A tiny hand waved.

Nat stretched her hand out cautiously, offering a finger.

Mildred seized it, burbling.

I am Nat. Natalayiana. SHiP. Shamanic drumming. Rob. Robyn. George –

'Robyn?' she murmured. 'Is Rob there?'

A hand stroked her exposed bottom.

'Should we get you a medical gown to wear at times?' Rob asked.

He leant over her, kissed the back of her head.

'Have you properly ploughed that lovely bottom yet?'

Rob laughed. 'Are you okay, Nat?'

Nat turned over slowly. Robyn was there, lifted Mildred up and away, smiling. Rob was there: put his arm around her, drew her into his embrace so she was leaning against him.

He stroked her gently. 'We were worried, Nat. You were mugged, concussed. They gave you something. You went into a coma –'

'A coma?'

Robyn sat down on the other side of the bed, unbuttoning her blouse so her daughter could feed. 'For three weeks. You occasionally dribbled, but that was the only sign of life.'

Her eyes were dark ringed. Rob's face was drawn.

'You both look – tired.' She reached up and stroked Rob's face. 'I've got so much to tell you.'

She felt Robyn's hand rest on her thigh. It felt comforting, no attempt to do anything other than touch her. She stroked, once, and withdrew it.

'Rob was so worried about you, he stopped being embarrassed about me feeding Mildred in front of him.'

She looked at him. 'Is this true?'

He nodded. 'You are all that matters, Nat.' He smiled. 'You'd crook your head turning to look, but Robyn's flashing us now.'

'Robyn?'

Robyn sighed. 'I'll put them away.'

Nat smiled, raising her hand to stroke Rob's chest. 'Not on my account. Rob likes busty women.'

Rob shrugged. 'So do you.' He grinned. 'But it's you I love, Nat.'

Nat blushed, laying her head against Rob's chest. 'Do the doctors want to see me? Can I go home yet?'

Rob stroked her back. 'They will be back in a while. I said we wanted some time with you first, but they know you're awake.'

Nat nodded. 'I love you, Rob.' She half turned her head. 'I love you, Robyn. And Mildred.'

She felt Robyn get onto the bed, and then her best friend was holding her as well. 'What happened – they said you were mugged?'

Nat nodded. 'I was in Blackbird Leys. I wasn't paying attention.'

Robyn winced.

'But you're okay?' Rob asked.

His hand lay over her heart. Nat nodded, kissing his neck.

The door opened. 'If we can have some time with the patient?'

--

'Well?' asked Rob, 'what did they say?'

Nat smiled at her lover. He still looked tired but his eyes were wide and he was grinning.

'Coffee?'

He chuckled, leaning in, kissing her.

Nat wrapped her arms around his shoulders, kissing him, holding him, glad she had him to cling on to. Glad – and happy – to beach herself on his shore any day.

Rob broke the kiss. Kissed her nose. Put an arm round her back to support her.

'Should I find you a medical gown? We could have fun. Would you like to play doctors and nurses?'

Nat sniggered. 'I wouldn't object to being a patient under your care, Doctor Adams.' She grinned. 'You would have to carry out deep examinations of me, regularly.'

Rob grinned, drawing her up against him, wrapping the quilt around her carefully. His hand slipped under it, until he could fondle and caress her.

'They've said you can come home tomorrow. They'll keep an eye on you overnight, make sure there's no lasting effects.'

Nat nodded, resting her hand on Rob's interest. 'Good.' She squeezed gently. 'I've so much,' she sighed, 'it feels like I haven't seen you for years.'

Rob grinned, shaking his head. 'Only three weeks. I've spoken to Bryan and Lord Merryweather. Bryan wants you to come in, but only a few hours each day. He said to say,' his brows darkened, 'George won't be in for a while.'

Nat felt a weight lift a little.

'Is it something I should know about?'

Nat shook her head. 'Yes. But not yet.' She stroked him. 'When can I – where's Robyn?'

'I sent Robyn and Mildred home, to ours. She'll get the house ready. The last few weeks,' he shrugged, ruefully.

'And Douglas? Lord Merryweather?'

Rob chuckled. 'He said he would like to visit you, when you're free. Or you can come round. He suggested Sunday.'

Nat nodded. She squeezed Rob. 'How long before I can have my not so little hedgehog inside me again?'

Rob chuckled. 'Doctor's orders are to rest the full weekend. Drink lots of water. Eat full meals.' He grinned. 'Maybe tomorrow evening, we'll see how you're feeling.'

Nat smiled. 'I do – want your Were to be comfortable with me. But not tomorrow. In general.'

Rob nodded. 'I know. I would like that. For my Were to get to know your scent properly.'

Nat grinned, kissing him again. 'There's more.'

'More?'

She nodded. 'I'm not sure I'll ever be comfortable with being fully naked in public. But I'd like to continue – doing things in the garden. And if we can find somewhere – outside – that's fairly quiet, I wouldn't object to doing a few things. And a little bit of humiliation.'

Rob smirked. 'One day, Nat, you will walk naked through a park and not care.'

Nat managed to resist shaking her head. 'I love you, Rob. Please continue – pushing my boundaries. After Clovis and Gerald –'

Rob drew her closer, his fingers stroking between her cheeks. 'You're okay with doing stuff in the garden. You're okay with Lucie and Gerald, you and I having a break somewhere and – exploring things. Being Were.'

Nat nodded.

'And you're not totally adverse,' he grinned, 'to being tied naked to a tree, somewhere deep in a forest, while I cane you and then take you from behind.'

Nat blushed. 'I almost think for that, we might have to rope in Lucie and Gerald to ensure – privacy.'

Rob chuckled. 'Threesome not enough for you?'

Nat's blush deepened. 'No, I meant, I really like that idea, and I do want us to do it, but if we were in the middle of it and were discovered – interrupted –' she shivered.

She squirmed as Rob moved his fingers intimately.

'Worse than getting fingered in a hospital ward?'

Saturday 7th May

Robyn wrapped her arms around her tightly, almost crushing her. Rob moved in behind, holding her, holding the pair of them.

'I'm okay,' she protested feebly, enjoying being squeezed between the pair of them.

'Of course you're okay,' Robyn almost purred, 'but we're glad you're safe. Don't do anything so foolish again. You know what Blackbird Leys is like.'

'I know,' Nat leant her head against Robyn's shoulder. She was acutely aware of Rob's interest and Robyn's bosom.

'I can leave you alone for a while, if you want,' Rob said.

Nat turned, awkwardly, in their embrace, forcing the pair of them to loosen their holds on her. 'No. Rob, you and I are an item. A couple. Robyn and I – are friends. She is our house guest. Nothing will happen between us – Robyn and I – unless we agree and it happens between all of us.'

'Do you want me to go?' Robyn asked.

Nat shook her head. 'No, Robyn. You're our friend. Staying here keeps you and Mildred safe from Dr Gold,' she shuddered, remembering being forced to undress by the doctor.

'What did she do to you?' Rob asked.

'Nothing.' She leaned up on tiptoe and kissed Rob. 'Well, something, but,' she took his hand. Took Robyn's as well. 'Robyn, I want you to stay tonight. You'll be on the sofa. Rob and I,' she blushed. 'Will be reacquainting ourselves with each other.'

Rob chuckled, tightening his grip on her hand.

'I need to – I want to make a couple of calls.' She looked at the pair of them. 'Will you arrange some deckchairs and some drinks outside, please. I only want water.'

Rob nodded. 'Of course.'

--

Nat showered quickly, having made the phone calls. All three of them smelled of the hospital, antiseptic and death. She glanced out the window: it was a cloudy day, with patches of sun, but warm. She could hear Rob and Robyn setting up the chairs.

Robyn – fucking Robyn is a treat. I can't let things just – happen with her. Maybe we should let her stay in the house and have a week away, just the two of us. I'd like that.

She pulled on knickers and a long skirt. Studied herself in the bathroom mirror, running fingers over her face lightly. I remember – passing out. Having my head slammed into the road. She shuddered. Bruises must have faded.

She grabbed a plain white slip and pulled it on, headed downstairs.

Three deckchairs had been set up and they'd left the middle one for her, a large bottle of water next to it. Robyn had her eyes closed, a drink in one hand and was rocking Mildred's cradle with her foot. Rob looked up at her and smiled.

Without even thinking about it she peeled her slip off and discarded it, sitting in Rob's lap. 'Hello,' she grinned.

He smiled appreciatively, pulling her down for a kiss. They kissed, her hands on his chest, his hands in her hair.

They broke apart eventually. 'Missed me?' she teased.

Rob nodded, licking his lips.

Later, she mouthed, standing up. She peeled the skirt off and discarded it. She sat in her deckchair, wriggling, trying to get comfortable. Her hair was a tangled, damp wave, irritating her slightly.

'Mmm,' Robyn murmured in appreciation. 'You could have given us a striptease, Nat.'

Nat smiled but didn't answer. It wasn't — *so* — scary. The neighbours across the way were probably out; it was mid-afternoon. If they weren't out in the garden already, they probably wouldn't be coming out. She was in just her knickers. It *was* her own garden.

Just her knickers. Her pants. With the man you love, she reminded herself. The man who loves you. The man you'll be doing wicked things with later.

With the woman you love, as well. The woman you fancy. The woman you want to fuck.

'Does anyone object,' Robyn asked, 'if I free the Devonshire pair for a while?'

Rob looked at her inquisitively. Tits, she mouthed, miming a chest. Rob grinned, lying back in his deckchair.

'Free them,' Nat smiled.

Robyn did. Nat tried not to look, but she was conscious of Robyn lying there, all swelling sun-lit curves.

'Robyn,' she asked, wriggling onto her side, 'how can you be so comfortable and confident naked?'

Robyn rolled onto her side. 'I don't care, Nat. I'm not bothered by what people think or say. You are.' She chuckled. 'You are lovely, Nat, and beautiful, and you shouldn't care what people think.'

Nat blushed. 'But they might see –'

Robyn shrugged. 'What if they do?'

'What if,' she asked hesitatingly, 'someone took photos?'

'If they asked,' Robyn grinned. She shrugged. 'Depends on who it was. I might let them. I might charge.'

Nat stared. 'You'd pose – nude?'

Robyn laughed. 'I have done before. I was in a calendar, years ago.'

Nat blinked. 'You never told me!'

Robyn sniggered. 'It was before I met you.'

Nat felt – disappointed.

Robyn chuckled. 'It wasn't full frontal or anything. I covered my hips, covered one tit, gave them one for free.'

She felt Rob's hand on her hip.

'Nat wants to know where she can find it.'

Nat blushed. 'I don –'

'I don't mind, Nat.' Rob chuckled. 'I'm not saying I wouldn't look, either.'

Robyn sat up. 'I had a copy of it. When I was evicted,' she shrugged. 'I'll look. I don't know if I've still got it. It was pre-internet.'

Rob ran his hand down her back. 'Is that something you'd consider, Nat?'

'A public – calendar? Besides,' she shrugged. 'They'd want people like Robyn, with chests and hips –'

Rob snorted. 'You've got a very nice arse, Nat. And a beautiful chest.'

'They'd want me to shave,' she protested.

Robyn lay back down. Mildred was just beginning to stir, and she started rocking her again.

'What if it was a private calendar?'

Nat turned to look at Rob. 'What do you mean?'

'I mean, there are people out there who do boudoir shoots. Or we could arrange something.'

Robyn lifted Mildred up and put her daughter to her breast. 'I've got some things I could lend you. If you want it kinky.'

Nat blushed.

'I need to have a shower,' Rob said. 'Would you like to join me, Nat? You look like you could do with cooling down.'

Nat glanced at Robyn, then Rob. 'Yes, please.' She glanced at Robyn, 'excuse us.'

Robyn stroked her daughter's head, chuckling quietly. 'Take your time. Take each other.'

--

Rob led her by the hand to the bathroom and slid the bolt home behind them.

'You like the idea of being in a calendar?'

Nat nodded. 'Yes. No. I like the idea, but I couldn't do a public one –'

'Sit on the edge of the bath.'

Nat sat. It was cold on her cheeks. She looked up at Rob.

He rolled his eyes, smiling. 'Nat, how am I going to eat you if you've got your knickers on?'

She blushed. 'Robyn's downstairs.'

Rob nodded. 'And it's you I want to eat. Nat,' he stroked her legs, 'my plan is to eat you, share a shower,' he grinned, 'and then have my way with you in the shower.'

Nat blushed, standing up, peeling her knickers down. Rob pulled her to him, kissing her, holding her tight.

'I was so worried,' he said softly. 'You didn't go into a coma straight away. You were unconscious, badly bruised –'

'Shush, shush,' she held him tight. 'I remember the attack, and then I was dreaming.' She kissed him then pushed him away. 'Lose the clothes then kneel before me. I am your Were goddess, after all,' she giggled.

Rob stripped and knelt before her, lifting her legs to put them on his shoulders, his arms going round her hips as he tucked in.

Nat leaned back, shifting, getting comfortable, bracing her hands against the wall, hoping she didn't fall *into* the bath while Rob did his thing.

His thing. She smiled. It's not just *his* thing – for an instant she was there, underwater, in the glass box – no, she was the water in the box. The *liquid* in the box.

Nat gasped, eyes crossing for a moment, as pleasure surged through her. There were wonderful dirty sounds of Rob snuffling at her like a truffle hound in heat. She drew her feet up, pushing her knees out, giving him even better access.

She moaned as he built up the pressure with his tongue. She was locked in position, slightly uncomfortable, losing control of her legs, unable to see because of the sweat in her eyes –

She shivered, feeling her skin burning, feeling goosebumps come and go, feeling – she thrust, awkwardly, losing control, hoping not to fall, but Rob held her tight.

Nat let out a long, contented chirrup at the end. Rob licked and she shivered, wanting to push him away, but her arms were locked.

'Help me up, Rob. I'm locked –'

He moved his hands and lifted her. She practically fell into his arms, sat on his lap, clutched at him, breathing heavily.

He chuckled, scratching her back.

'That's the best orgasm I've had,' she blushed, 'for a while.'

Rob smirked. 'Ready for a shower?'

She shook her head. 'I can't stand up. My legs have gone.' She stroked his interest. 'You could just take me to bed and have me.'

Rob grinned, shaking his head. 'Oh, no. We'll shower. I want to take you in the shower.'

Nat smiled, laying her head against his chest. 'We can talk tomorrow. We've got guests coming round. But now,' she managed to stand up, wobbling, feeling unsteady on her feet.

Rob grabbed her hips. 'Now we shower you.' He grinned. 'Are you up to –'

Nat stroked his arm. 'Let's get in the shower and get you inside me.'

She stepped into the bath, one hand on the wall for support. Rob leaned past her, turning the shower on and the water came through, stinging, cold, and she gasped.

He held her in place, hard against her arse, and the water warmed up rapidly. 'Oh, Nat,' he murmured.

She turned: Rob leaned forward and around her, putting his hands underneath her arse and lifting her, holding her against the wall. Nat wrapped her legs around him as tightly as she could.

'Go on, Mr Hedgehog,' she smiled, 'have your wicked way with me.'

Sunday 8th May

'It's not like you to wear knickers, Nat.'

Nat stuck her tongue out at Rob. He sprawled deliciously – and deliberately – naked in bed, his interest evident.

'Alice and Howard will be round shortly. Robyn's said her goodbyes and gone. I'm not – normally – the first one up.'

Rob chuckled. 'I am up,' he grinned. 'Three times in an evening is very good going.'

Nat picked up the short-skirted purple dress, one of her favourites. Full sleeved and buttoned to the neck, but only mid-thigh. It was lovely, but she couldn't show Alice, nor her fiancée Howard, and certainly not Douglas, who was coming round in the afternoon, just how hairy her legs were, fine though the hair was. She wriggled into it, reaching for a pair of tights.

'Like a striptease gone wrong,' Rob grinned.

Nat looked at him. 'I don't think there's any risk of you not getting to take the tights and knickers down later.' She pulled the tights up carefully. 'I certainly intend to sit on your face and ride you, but I'm not risking accidentally flashing Alice and Howard or Douglas.'

Rob grinned, reaching for her.

Nat batted his hands away. 'Later, Rob. Alice is my friend and this is the first time I've met Howard. They're getting married in August; I'll be organising Alice's stag party and giving her away.'

'Brides –'

'Alice liked the sound of a stag party.' She leant in and kissed him. 'We will have a good time fucking tonight, Rob,' and she slipped her hand round his interest, coaxing him a little, 'but now it's time to get up and dressed.'

He groaned but grinned, rolling out of bed quickly as she began buttoning up her dress.

--

'I hope it wasn't inconvenient, Alice. I know you had to miss working with the conservation volunteers; and I'm sorry it was such short notice, but –'

Alice almost ran to her and hugged her tightly. 'Are you okay? Tomas enquired; they said you'd been in a comma.'

'A coma,' Nat smiled, 'but won't you introduce me to your young man.'

Alice blushed. Howard was dark haired and a couple of inches taller than Alice, with a thickset body. His trousers were too long and held up with a belt; he wore a fading cardigan over a shirt and tie. He smiled awkwardly.

'This is Howard,' she smiled sweetly at him.

Howard nodded, looking a little over-awed.

'Please, take a seat both.' She glanced at Rob. 'This is Robert. Rob. My other half. Can I offer either of you a drink – tea or squash, perhaps?'

Alice nodded. 'Squash. Howard likes squash, don't you?'

Howard nodded, smiling innocently.

'We don't,' Alice blushed, 'we haven't,' she hesitated.

'I'll sort some drinks,' Rob grinned, inclining his head and withdrawing tactfully.

'It's not the same without you there,' Alice almost wailed.

'I've never,' Howard spoke, looking around. 'My parents. I don't,' he trailed off.

'It's okay,' Nat smiled at them both. 'I had an accident. Was in a coma for a while, which is why I wasn't at the conservation group. I'm going to an event next weekend, but I'll be back after that, Alice.'

Alice nodded happily. 'Oh,' she looked up, 'I have to get a wedding dress. Will you help me pick a wedding dress, Nat?'

'You look nice,' said Howard, awkwardly, to Alice.

Nat nodded. 'Of course. I need to go into work tomorrow, they want me to ease back in slowly, so I'm sure I'll have time this week, if that's okay?'

Alice nodded.

'Are you nervous about the wedding, Alice? It's May now; it'll soon be August.'

Alice nodded again, blushing, looking at Howard. 'I'm looking forward to it.'

Howard nodded. 'Where will we live?'

Alice smiled brightly, too brightly. 'Somewhere. Your parents will let us stay for a while, I'm sure. Or my place might,' she trailed off.

Nat nodded. 'It's a longshot, but I know someone I can ask. They might at least tell me what the chances are to get you housed if your place won't let you stay, Alice.'

Alice beamed. 'Thank you, Natalie.' She seemed to hesitate. 'Did I pronounce that right? You have a strange name.'

Nat laughed. 'You can stick with Nat, Alice. Most people call me Nat as opposed to Natalayiana.'

'Did your mother call you Natanna,' Alice stumbled awkwardly over the name, 'when you did something wrong?'

Nat pulled a face. 'My mother didn't think much of me,' she smiled up at Rob as he returned with a tray of soft drinks and plates of biscuits.

He put them on the table in front of Alice and Howard and sat on the arm of the chair next to her.

'They told Nat not to rush or exert herself for a while, otherwise I'm sure she would have wanted to be there this morning.'

He put his hand on her shoulder, a warm, comforting touch.

'My parents call me How Ard when I've done something wrong,' said Howard.

'I like How Ard,' Alice breathed, a warmth in her eyes.

'My sister always called me Robert if I did anything she didn't like. She brought me up.'

'Kelly – my step-mum – would always put her head on her side and look at me quizzically.'

Rob stroked her shoulder.

'Nat said you wanted a stag party, before your wedding, Alice?'

Alice nodded, blushing. 'I haven't – there wouldn't be anyone but,' she lowered her voice a little, 'Nat and I.'

'You can have a stag party for two people,' Rob smiled, stroking her shoulder. 'Howard, would you like to have a pre-wedding party as well?'

Howard looked up, surprised and nervous. 'I,' he hesitated. 'I don't really know anyone.'

Nat put her hand on Rob's hand grateful for his support. 'Would your father come? What about a best man?'

Howard blinked. 'Best man.' He pulled a face. 'I don't know.'

'Would you like to,' she glanced up at Rob, 'maybe a dinner party. I could invite a few people.'

Howard looked at Alice.

'I don't know,' Alice began, 'many people –'

'How about my colleague Marianne, and my – our – friend Robyn?'

'Robyn,' Rob said, 'is a young mother. She hasn't got many people in her life. And her daughter Mildred is no problem.'

Nat nodded. 'And Marianne's,' she smiled, 'a grandmother sort of person. But you don't have to decide right now, or if you think that's more than you could cope with –'

Alice smiled shyly. 'I would like that.' She looked at Howard. 'We would like that.'

--

Lord Merryweather wrapped his arms around her and hugged her gently.

'I am delighted to see you up and about, Nat. I was worried about you. It sounded – horrendous. Bad.'

Nat smiled. Douglas smelled – reassuringly solid. And of cigarettes.

'Still smoking?'

He raised an eyebrow. 'It would be worse to stop now, dear Nat. But that's not why we're here.'

He took a seat at the end of the sofa nearest her. The end that, not a few months ago, Rob had put her over and spanked; had put strawberry ice cream into her. She squirmed, trying not to blush at the memory.

'Are you alright, Nat?'

She nodded, subsiding. 'I,' she hesitated. 'I wanted to thank you for – the offer.'

'Offer?'

'Clovis. Merryweather Hall.'

Douglas nodded. 'And?'

Nat smiled, looking up at Rob. 'And of course I'm going to accept. I am – honoured – that you trust me with your future.' She blushed. 'I mean, Merryweather Hall. And Clovis.'

Douglas chuckled. 'Good. I am delighted. I hope you were not upset about my asking – the last time we met?'

'Was I a Were?' Nat breathed, remembering.

Douglas nodded. 'I had to ask. And I am sorry if it raked over your – past.'

Nat managed to smile. 'A lot has happened since then.'

'You slept for three weeks,' Rob smiled.

Nat shook her head. 'Well, yes. But no. I dreamed.'

He raised an eyebrow. 'I didn't tell you Rob, because,' she half smiled. 'I don't know why. But I knew I wanted Douglas – Lord Merryweather – to hear it.'

'I would be delighted to hear it,' he replied, settling back on the sofa with the coffee Rob had brought him, 'but please, my name is Douglas, not Lord Merryweather.'

Nat blushed. 'I sometimes – it's not that I forget, but I don't want to seem presumptuous. You're a lord, I'm a –'

'My ancestors were thieves and bullies. You've got the biggest heart of anyone I know, Natalayiana. I am the one who is honoured to know you.'

Nat stared, feeling suddenly exquisitely sad, tears trickling down her cheeks.

Rob was there, and she pressed her face to his chest, his arms wrapping around her shoulders. She clung to him for a moment, trying not to sob, wondering why she was so emotional.

'Oh, my dear almost-daughter, I did not mean to make you cry. Shall I go, and stop putting my feet in my mouth when I talk to you?'

Nat shook her head, pushing Rob away gently. 'No, please.' She sniffed, wiping her eyes. 'I'm emotional. Tired.'

'Well, I am glad you are out of the coma and alright, Nat. This discussion can wait; I can start matters with your say so, though we will need to get some documents signed in front of witnesses.'

Nat nodded. 'Thank you,' she smiled. 'But I did want to talk to you. A kind-of favour to ask.'

Douglas nodded. 'Of course. Name it, anything I can give, anything I can do.'

'I have heard,' she smiled at Rob, 'you talk to people. You bring people together.'

Douglas nodded. 'Yes. It is one of life's joys, creating conversation between people of disparate viewpoints.'

'It,' she sighed, 'it might only have been a coma-dream, but it felt real. I wandered if you,' she shook her head. 'No. It's silly. Just a dream.'

'What was the dream, Nat?' Rob asked, rubbing her back softly.

'Nothing is silly, Nat,' Douglas said, 'sometimes, there is a link or some connection between what a person in a coma dreams, and what is going on around them at the time.'

Nat nodded slowly. 'It felt so – real. I was in the depths of the ocean. There was a glass box.'

'What was in the box?' Rob asked.

She shook her head. 'Just water. Liquid. I don't know,' she shrugged. 'But I know it was too deep in the ocean, the pressure was too intense for anything – to be alive.'

Douglas nodded. 'I will ask around. Robert, were there any issues around Nat's breathing while she was in the coma? Lung issues?'

Rob shook his head. 'I don't think so. She went into a coma really quickly and either I or Robyn was there the whole time.' He stroked Nat's hair. 'Just a coma. Nothing – life threatening. But no guarantees you'd come out alive.'

Nat nodded, looking away. 'I'm sorry. It was silly. But,' she shook her head. Her hand turning into a paw. Lucie's face becoming a skull. And now observing water in a box in the depths of the ocean.

'It wasn't silly,' said Douglas, 'since it's obviously on your mind. I'll ask around.' He smiled. 'I do not wish to put any more stress on you, Nat. I will take my leave of you.'

'You don't have to,' she protested.

He smiled, putting his cup down on the table. 'I will be around on Thursday; I believe you are meeting Clovis on Thursday?'

Nat nodded. 'Yes.'

He grinned. 'I will likely see you then.'

--

'How are you feeling, Nat?'

She looked up. Looked around. Evening light was slanting through the front window.

'Douglas?' she frowned, half sitting up.

Rob gently pushed her back into the chair. 'You said goodbye. He left hours ago. You flaked out.'

'I meant what I said, Rob. I saw – no, I think I *was* the water. It's something important. That box, that glass,' she sighed, feeling a little light headed.

'I think you need to have some water and then be put to bed.'

Nat frowned. 'I was going to ride you. I want to ride you.'

He grinned. Leant in and kissed her forehead. 'If you're going in to the office tomorrow, don't be more than a couple of hours. If Bryan doesn't like it,' he almost growled.

'You can't threaten my boss,' she protested, half grinning.

Rob smiled, kneeling before her. 'Nobody hurts my Were goddess. Can you walk upstairs or should I carry you?'

'You *could* take my tights and knickers down. I wouldn't object to being eaten by my hedgehog prince.'

Rob stood up, putting his arms under her knees and back, lifting her almost effortlessly. 'I'm going to take you upstairs, Nat. I will take your tights and knickers off you then lock up the house. If you're still awake after,' he grinned.

'Of course I'll still be awake,' Nat protested.

He carried her up to their bedroom. Drew the covers down and placed her in the bed. Slipped his hands beneath her skirt and drew down her knickers and tights.

'Five minutes and I'll be back,' he promised.

Nat nodded, closing her eyes. She was safe. The *ocean* was safe. Whatever the liquid was, it was safely contained in the glass box.

Monday 9th May

Nat was almost smothered in Marianne's embrace.

'Should you be in?' Marianne asked, giving Nat room to breathe.

Nat nodded. 'I'm not in all day. I've got to see the Police later, give them my evidence, what I remember,' she looked away for an instant. Not that I remember much. 'I need to build my strength up. I get tired, very easily. I fell asleep mid-afternoon in the chair. I even,' she blushed.

'Even?' Marianne raised an eyebrow.

'I was on a promise. Fell asleep in a five minute window.'

Marianne laughed. 'Oh, it's not funny. But it is.' She smiled. 'It's good to see you.' She shook her head. 'There's been some changes here.'

'George?'

Marianne frowned at her. 'George is – he handed his notice in. Bryan won't accept it, so he's suspended for a month. He'll only come back on the proviso,' she shook her head. 'Bryan will tell you all.'

'And – Thomas?'

Marianne sniggered. 'He's still here.'

Nat pulled a face.

Marianne smirked. 'Close to cracking. He's doing the work of the three of you. It seems,' she lowered her voice, 'I do wonder whether some of the – recommendations – were talking him up. He doesn't have

183

your or George's finesse.' She frowned. 'What happened
– with George?'

Nat shook her head. 'He,' she hesitated.

'Nat!' Bryan appeared in the doorway. 'You're
here. I wasn't sure whether to expect you this week or
not.'

'She's only in for a few hours, Bryan,' Marianne
spoke waspishly. 'She has not long awoken from a three
week coma.'

'I know,' Bryan scowled at Marianne. 'I'm not
totally inhuman, Marianne. Would you like to come
through, Nat, and we'll have a talk?'

Nat nodded. 'Yes. See you later, Marianne.'

Bryan held the door open for her. The inner office
– was a tip. The desks overflowed with files, including
stacked up on the floor and overflowing from their piles.
The air wasn't fresh. Bryan, himself, looked tired, his eyes
ringed grey.

'This – doesn't look good.'

Bryan nodded. Sighed, gestured to his office.

'Sit.' He sat. 'It's a mess, Nat. Were Legal
Opportunities,' he shook his head. 'They just keep piling
work onto us. You're off, I presume not back full time this
week. Next week?'

Nat shrugged. 'I don't know, Bryan. I need to drink
a lot, rest, rebuild my strength. Definitely not full time this
week.'

He nodded. 'Okay. That's kind of what I thought.
What,' he hesitated. 'What happened with George?'

Nat shook her head. 'He wasn't himself. I think this – thing – with Evie – has him really distracted. He loves her and they've been going out for – decades.'

'He said he made a move on you.'

'O.'

'O, indeed.'

Nat sighed. 'Nothing happened.'

Bryan raised an eyebrow.

'Well, okay,' she admitted, 'he pinned me to a desk, almost made a move on me, said no one would know if – we did anything.'

Bryan scowled. Shook his head. 'He wanted to resign. I said no.' He sighed. 'He's been riding you pretty hard, hasn't he? Um,' he realised, 'I mean –'

Nat nodded. 'So did Thomas. So did you. You supported, encouraged them.'

Bryan looked away. 'Thomas,' he scowled, 'is not coping. Were Legal Opportunities found him – indirectly – but I really don't think he's up to the job.'

Nat smiled, a little. 'You need me back as a caseworker.'

Bryan sighed. 'Honestly, at the moment, Nat,' he sighed even deeper. 'I'm almost wondering is it even worth it.'

Nat stared. 'You can't mean that! Without us –'

Bryan shook his head. 'There is no us, Nat. SHiP cannot contractually deliver what WLO want. You're capable but out of the loop, I have,' he shook his head. 'George is out for the next couple of weeks, at least. He's doing some courses. Anger management. I think he's trying to get back together with –'

'Evie.'

Bryan nodded. 'Marriage guidance, though I don't know. Thomas,' he shrugged. 'He might be able to turn it around, but I'm having my doubts.' He frowned. 'He was too good to be true.'

Nat remembered – undressing before Dr Gold. Being put over her desk. The doctor was on the board of Were Legal Opportunities. Had thoroughly enjoyed using a wooden ruler to punish her. I haven't even told Rob that. I could barely sit through the drumming.

But Lae – *she* – enjoyed disciplining me. If I offered myself to her – freely – might she be able to free SHiP from the contract?

It's not my business. Not my company.

I don't see Bryan being successful in offering himself to her.

She wouldn't want him.

It's my job, not my company. I don't have to –

If you don't, who will. If SHiP folds –

There is Douglas. He would ensure I was – okay.

I'm not a charity case.

She sighed. 'I – *might* – be able to sort something. No promises, Bryan. But I know someone on the board of Were Legal Opportunities.'

He stared at her in surprise. 'Who? How? Why?'

She smiled tightly. 'No promises.'

Bryan shook his head. 'That would help, Nat. There's no guarantees. At the moment,' he seemed to draw himself together. 'Are you going to see Jezabel later?'

Nat nodded. 'Yes. She won't like that I didn't tell her –'

'I posted a note to her. I didn't want to – lose the work you'd already done with her.'

Nat nodded. 'Thank you.'

--

Nat was engulfed in the embrace of a big-busted squirrel-furry.

'Naaaaat!' screamed Jezabel, hugging her tightly, ramming her costume-enhanced bosom into Nat's face and holding her tightly.

Nat coughed and choked, breathing in the scent of an unwashed body full of pheromones, and a squirrel costume adorned with the remnants of too many meals.

'Nat!' Jezabel almost screamed again. 'I thought you were dead. Or you didn't care.'

She was hugged and squeezed again, almost lifted off her feet, and still only in the doorway of Jezabel's flat.

'Jezabel! Jezabel,' she managed, trying not to cough.

She was put back on her feet and Jezabel drew her in, closing the door behind her.

'What happened? I thought you had died! They said you were in hospital, and then nothing. I thought you had changed your mind about the convention.'

Nat shook her head, trying not to flare her nostrils at the strong, overlapping smells. 'I was mugged. Knocked out. Went to hospital and then went into a coma. Did you get the message from SHiP?'

She nodded. 'Yes. But then nothing more. I thought,' she trailed off, slumping down into her favourite chair.

'You thought I was trying to avoid you? I would never do that to anyone.'

Jezabel sighed. 'Others have. An ex told me he couldn't go out with me because his hand had been chopped off. I saw him later, both hands over another woman.'

Nat shook her head. 'I would never do that, Jezabel.'

Jezabel nodded slowly.

'When did you last –' she shook her head – 'that costume looks like it needs a wash.'

Jezabel shrugged. 'I've been in it for three weeks.'

'Do you think you should wash it before you wear it to the convention?'

Jezabel looked up at her. 'Why are you going to the convention, Nat? You've got a partner, you're not looking for a fuck buddy. You don't strike me as a furry, though I don't know what your kink is.'

'My – kink?'

'Everyone has one. I used to really like modelling, naked for preference. Now,' she shrugged. 'Now I just want to get a cock inside me. What about you, Nat? Why are you going to the convention?'

'To support you.'

Jezabel pulled a face. 'Please. No one is that nice. What's your real reason?'

Nat looked away.

Jezabel laughed. 'You want someone who'll be there.'

'No, of course not,' Nat looked back at Jezabel. 'Well,' she hesitated.

Jezabel crowed. 'What's his name?'

Nat shook her head. 'Her. Daiandrea. She's the organiser. She gave me two free tickets when I said I was interested in going.'

'Nat and Daiandrea, sitting on a tree,' Jezabel crowed, 'F. I. N. G. E. R. I. N. G.'

Nat blushed. 'No,' the thought, the always present thought, image, when she thought about Daiandrea, was of herself, naked, lying on her back, Daiandrea standing above her, rubbing her belly with her foot. She was purring like a contented cat; like a well satisfied pussy.

--

Nat showered the moment she got in. Rob was out; had left her a note saying he wouldn't be long, had gone to do some shopping.

She wrapped her hair up in a towel and ransacked her drawers, looking for a specific slip. I'll tell Rob about – Dr Gold. The caning. She blushed. Then he can – we can – she found the slip she was after and pulled it on, tugging

189

it past the towel before going back to look at herself in the bathroom mirror.

The slip was perfect, a pale creamy-gold. It was tight; if she'd had any kind of bust, it would have been unwearable. It was short enough that it didn't reach her hips, leaving her totally exposed.

She went downstairs, hearing the key in the lock, and went through to the kitchen.

Rob came through a minute later, putting the bags down and wolf-whistling appreciatively. He grabbed her cheeks, nuzzling her neck.

'That's a nice sight to come home to,' he grinned, 'how was today?'

'I've got something to tell you,' Nat forced herself to say. 'Something you might want to – discipline me over.'

He pushed her up against the kitchen table, hard against her, one hand on her belly, the other pulling her slip down, fingers slipping inside.

'What have you done, Natalayiana?' he asked, warmth in his voice.

'Before the accident, Dr Gold summoned me to see her. The day I went shamanic drumming.'

She felt Rob nod, his fingers tweaking and teasing her nipple.

'The night before, I'd gone round to Robyn. Nothing happened, Rob, but we were – sunbathing. Nude.'

Rob chuckled again, his other hand sliding down, fingers burrowing into her fur. 'So far I'm enjoying this.'

Nat nodded. 'Dr Gold came round to take Robyn and Mildred in. We didn't see her.'

'And she didn't take them in?'

Nat shook her head. 'No. She summoned me.'

'And you were just sunbathing?'

Nat shook her head. 'No. Yes.' She sighed. 'No. We got to talking. I was –' she sighed. 'It was a little bit like role play. Robyn was maternal. I was thirsty.'

Rob's finger pushed between her lips and she yelped.

'You were drinking her milk, nothing else?'

Nat nodded. 'Yes. She cuddled me, afterwards. I lay on top of her, my head on her chest.'

'Did you come?' he asked softly.

Nat shook her head.

'Did Robyn come?'

Nat shook her head.

'Nat.' Rob kissed the back of her head. 'I do think – sometimes – we should cut Robyn out of our lives. Just for a while. Or,' and he pushed his finger a little deeper into her. 'We should just make it an open, three way, relationship.'

'It's you I love, Rob. You I want.'

'Have you told Robyn you're a Were?'

She shook her head. 'We can't cut her out and tell her. That would be to abandon her. And Dr Gold will do all sorts of things to her and Mildred.'

She could feel Rob nodding.

'What did Doctor Gold want? Do?'

She hesitated. I should tell him. He's already annoyed. I don't want to upset him –

A second finger was pushed, a little crudely, into her and she yelped. Rob was holding her tightly.

'Tell me the truth, Nat.'

'Dr Gold – asked if I was a Were. She knows you are. She knows, obviously, that Mildred is the daughter of a Were. She said Weres were attracted, formed bonds, with other Weres.'

'And?'

'And she threated to take it out on Robyn.'

'What did she do?'

'She,' Nat trembled. 'She made me strip. Put me over her desk. Used a ruler on me.'

'Oh?'

'I mean,' Nat was almost crying, 'she struck me with a ruler until it hurt to sit down. She likes – hurting me. Humiliating me.'

Rob released her and she staggered, almost fell, but Rob caught her. He wrapped his arms tightly around her and lowered her to the ground so that she was lying in his lap.

'I should be annoyed,' he almost smiled, 'but I'm more concerned about you. Nat,' he sighed. Kissed her forehead. 'I love you deeply. You care about everyone deeply. I wish you didn't, at times,' he made a rueful face.

'You want me to – cut Robyn out?'

He shook his head. 'No, Nat.' He stroked her arm gently. 'I'm sorry if I was a little crude. Forceful.'

Nat smiled weakly. 'You should probably – discipline me.'

Rob shook his head. 'No, Nat.' He forced a grin. 'Well, yes, but not now.' He drew her more into his embrace.

Nat snuggled in against him.

'We will be okay, won't we?' she asked, when the silence became too much.

He nodded. 'We will be.' He smiled gently. 'Draw your slip down.'

Nat obeyed, feeling shy, feeling like she was undressing before him for the first time.

'You are beautiful, Nat. Not just your body, but your heart, your soul, as well. I am honoured to be here with you.' He smiled, and a wicked glint came into his eyes. 'Is it wrong that I want to make you come into my hand?'

Nat smiled shyly. 'We should have a date night. We could call this a date night. And since it's our fourth or fifth date at least, I'm hoping – at the very least – you'll finger me.'

Tuesday 10ᵗʰ May

Nat stared. It was – breathtakingly beautiful. A wedding dress of lace and silk, so fine, crystalline, almost like a spider's web, frozen in a state of perfection –

'Um. It is beautiful, Alice.'

Alice beamed at her. 'So soft. So nice.' She giggled. 'I can't wait for Howard to see me in it.'

Nat nodded. 'I am sure he would enjoy it. Is it expensive?'

Alice breathed in.

Nat hardly dared look, grateful that the assistant was leaving them alone.

'It is. But's it's lovely. Don't I look like a princess!'

Alice twirled, but it was a slightly clumsy twirl.

'You do, Alice,' Nat smiled. 'You're getting married in a church, aren't you?'

Alice nodded happily.

'Yes.'

'The, um, priest, vicar, whatever it is, may have an issue if you wear that dress.'

'Why?' Alice frowned. 'It's lovely! A fairy tale princess dress.'

'It is beautiful, Alice, and so are you.'

Alice nodded. 'See. I can wear it.'

'I know it is your special day –'

'It is!' she beamed happily. 'And only a few months away. Weeks.'

'Um, the issue is,' Nat tried again.

Alice smiled. Breathed in. 'Do you not like it because you can see my breasts?'

Nat blinked. 'I do like it, Alice. But the lace on the bodice is quite – revealing.'

Alice breathed in, deliberately deeply, again. 'It's lovely,' she looked down at herself. 'I'm lovely. They're lovely.' She looked up at Nat. 'Are you jealous because you haven't got any?'

Nat stared. Shook her head. 'No. In that, Alice, the vicar will see pretty much the whole of your chest. So will everyone in the congregation. Is it – appropriate?'

Alice stared at her. Blinked. And burst into tears.

Wednesday 11th May

Nat knocked on the door, glancing up and down the curving corridor as she did so. 'Hello?'

'Who is it?' the voice within was cautious.

'Miss Harewood. Natalayiana.'

She was in the council officers, on an upper level. It was a terribly aged building that had, no doubt, been thought of as trendy and with-it when an architect had suggested it. There were no formal levels; the whole building led off a magnificent and unnecessarily large spiralling corridor that wound up and up until it reached a roof garden. Offices led off the ramp at regular intervals but there was no clear delineation between floors.

The door opened.

'Nat!' beamed Uriah; counsellor Barnet. 'Come in.'

He stepped back into the room, ushering her in and closing the door behind her. Gestured to a chair.

'Thank you.' Nat waited as he returned to his seat. 'I don't know – if this is you. If you can help,' she sighed. 'I could probably find out from the main desk –'

'Ask,' he interrupted her, 'ask, Nat, whatever it is. The worst, I can say no.'

Nat nodded. 'Thank you.' She blushed. 'It's a housing situation. For a friend of mine.'

'Go on.'

'Her name is Alice Maine. She lives in,' she gave the name of Alice's accommodation.

Uriah nodded. 'I am aware of it. I am not actually a council official, but I can make enquiries. What is the issue?'

Nat half smiled. 'She is getting married. They say she cannot stay once she is married; the parents of the man she is marrying will throw him out as well once they're married.'

Uriah nodded, settling back a little into his chair. 'You could have asked at reception, but you would not have got very far, Nat. Enquiries *should* be made by either of the parties directly or a close family member. However,' he grinned. 'I do know there are a couple of places that may be able to take a married couple. I presume, being in,' he hesitated.

Nat nodded. 'I've never asked – what. Alice holds down a job and does voluntary work.'

Uriah nodded. 'I can ask. And I will put some weight behind it.' He smiled.

'Thank you.'

He shook his head. 'I would not hold out hope, Nat. If Alice is able to work, and her husband can –'

'But if they're both thrown out of their homes –'

Uriah smiled. 'I can have someone find the appropriate forms in advance. If both are thrown out – and something can be obtained from both parties' landlords, hopefully, confirming they will be evicted when they are married – when are they getting married?'

'August.'

He nodded. 'The council has a duty to rehouse them. It may not be the best of areas, or the largest of properties, but a property will be found.'

'You can – pull strings – that easily?'

Uriah chuckled. 'It is not pulling strings. I used to work for the council, long before I became a councillor. I know how the system works. I know who does the work, who makes the decisions.' He smiled. 'All perfectly legal.' He shrugged. 'Mostly.'

'Thank you.'

The councillor shook his head. 'Do not thank me, Nat.' He sat forwards, growing serious. 'I had been meaning to have a word with you, anyway.'

'Oh?'

He smiled. 'Relax. It is nothing onerous or bad. I think. Maybe.'

Nat nodded. 'What is it?'

Uriah started to speak; his eyes darted to the door. He drew back; shook his head. 'Can you meet me next week, Nat?'

She nodded. 'Of course. Where and when?'

He shook his head. 'I'll let you know.'

--

It was raining by the time Nat got in, a light summer rain. The deckchairs were still up in the garden: she got the golfing umbrellas out and put them up, shading the chair – mostly – from the rain.

If I think about this –

She removed her blouse and slip, leaving them on the back of a chair. Picked up the book she'd been reading and a bottle of water and headed out.

The rain made a comforting patter-patter on the umbrella. By drawing her legs up, she could avoid getting her feet wet, though occasional drips snuck between the umbrellas.

She opened the book and laid it on her chest. It was – liberating and daft and –

And quite peaceful, she realised. The house was locked; only Rob could get in. The patio couldn't be overlooked by the neighbours on either side, and though the garden abutted the end of the neighbour's garden opposite, the rain would keep them out of theirs.

Nat blushed. 'Get me,' she whispered. 'Topless in my own garden.'

She sat back, wriggling, trying to get even more comfortable on the damp chair.

After a moment she gave up. The sound of the rain and the dampness in the air was soporific.

I'll go and see Alice next week. Make sure she's okay. She sighed. I think she understood that dress – she blushed. I could see her nipples. It'd be a nice treat for Howard, but to wear as a wedding gown –

Why shouldn't she wear it as a wedding gown? It was beautiful white lace.

She was practically topless in it. For her own wedding. It's a bit much –

It's not your decision, she argued with herself.

She would be shamed, wearing that.

Who would shame her?

It was a beautiful dress, she said to herself. If I had the figure for it – and wanted to get married – she shook her head. I'd wear it with something over the top. Take it off for my husband or wife to –

Husband or wife?

Yes, she argued, silently, with herself. I love Rob. I love Robyn. She sighed. I don't want to let Rob down, but the idea of an open relationship with Robyn –

She bit her lip. Robyn doesn't know you're a Were. She doesn't know Rob's a Were. If she found out – if she gets pregnant from what we – from what *Rob* did – I was happy for Rob to fuck her. Robyn *needs* to be taken care of.

But if she's pregnant –

'Hello?'

'Out here Rob,' she grinned as she heard him approach.

'Are you –' he stuck his head round the umbrella. 'Nice,' he grinned.

She smiled shyly. 'It's quite nice, under here. You should join me.'

Rob raised an eyebrow. 'Frankly, I think I'm quite overdressed.'

Nat nodded. 'You wouldn't be overdressed in just your pants.'

He grinned. 'Am I going to be lying on top or underneath you?'

'Underneath,' Nat blushed. She lowered the book. 'Don't take too long undressing.'

He licked his lips. 'Nice.' Disappeared back inside.

If Robyn is pregnant – If Robyn's pregnant then *I'm* responsible. Rob might have been the one – and we don't know she is, anyway. But if she is, then I have to shield her from Dr Gold. And tell her we're Were.

Rob reappeared, suitably dressed in just his pants. Nat licked her lips, sitting up and shifting about as he manoeuvred onto the deckchair beneath her.

'I think you're the overdressed one now, Nat. Lose the trousers.'

'I'd be in just my knickers,' she protested.

Rob took the book from her. 'It's raining, Nat. We're not quite letting our Weres run wild, but we're building up to that. Weres – are creatures of nature. Let some of that wildness in, Nat.' He grinned. 'Besides, think how good it'll be sat in my lap in just your knickers.'

Nat blushed. Unzipped.

'Good. Now I've got you undressing, how was today?'

'I went to see Uriah,' she half turned her head to smile at him, unbuckling her belt. 'Councillor Barnet. Trying to get accommodation for Alice and Howard before the wedding and they get thrown out.'

Rob sat up, an arm round her shoulder, drawing her in for a quick kiss. 'How are *you* feeling? Tired, thirsty? And more strange dreams?'

Nat shook her head. 'I can still remember it — clearly. So strange,' she pushed her trousers down, wriggling out of them. 'I feel like I'm at the seaside.'

Rob grinned, drawing her back down so she lay on top of him, trapping her wrists by her sides.

'Is the world ending, Nat?'

She could feel him, hard against her. The rain felt fresher, everything felt – brighter. Not quite scarier – but then she was sunbathing in the rain in her garden with her boyfriend, wearing nothing but a pair of knickers.

'No,' she admitted, feeling a frisson of delight and slight cold.

'If you're cold, Nat,' he threatened, 'we're going in and I'm putting you to bed in a dressing gown.'

'I would like that,' she said, 'but not yet.' She closed her eyes, leaning her head against his shoulder.

He released her wrists, wrapping his arms around her belly. It was snug, being held in his embrace.

'The next time we do this,' he spoke softly, 'you'll be lying face down on me and we'll have you naked.' He stroked her chest. 'Do you like that idea?'

Nat nodded. 'It would have to be in the rain. We'd be hidden, shielded. I could do it then.'

Rob chuckled. 'One day I will get you to walk naked through a field or park, Nat, and it won't matter in the least.'

'One day,' she murmured. She sat up. 'Possibly –'

Rob stroked her back.

'I would like,' she hesitated.

'Ask.'

Nat blushed. 'I do want to know more about being a Were. About how it works with Gerald and Lucie.'

'Similar to how it works with you and I, I should imagine. Except Lucie can't change.'

Nat nodded. 'I mean, I know he's my ex and she's your sister –'

Rob nodded. 'Lucie's made it clear she would like to watch the two of us together. And she would like to make me watch her fucking – being with – you.'

Nat blushed. 'We have to – talk about it properly. In advance.'

Rob nodded, stroking her back and drawing her back down into his embrace. 'Would you be happy for it to get kinky?'

Nat shivered. Blushed. 'I would.' She smiled shyly. 'But I would like to talk, as well. I feel – horny – a lot of the time. Is that from – being a Were?'

Rob chuckled, using his fingernails on her back, making her shiver and shudder. 'It's from being young and alive.'

Nat turned so she was lying on top of him. 'Yes but no. I spent so long with Clovis, with Gerald,' she hesitated.

'You want to fuck everything that breathes?'

Nat blushed. 'Not quite. But yes. Am I bad? I think of Laetitia and Robyn. I try not to think of Laetitia, but –'

Rob stopped her with a kiss. Kissed her until she stopped trying to speak. 'You're not bad, Nat. But we probably could line up some light discipline for you.'

'Light?' she tried not to be disappointed.

'The last time you changed, remember.' He grinned. 'Although I did quite enjoy taming your Were and having her.'

Nat blushed. Shook her head slightly. 'She would have liked you to have been bigger. And Were. She needs to be dominated fully, and a human can't.'

Rob nodded. 'She is far wilder and more feral than you are.' He stroked her chest. 'I think next time I will put you over my lap and tan your bare bottom with my hand. So much more intimate if discipline is delivered by hand.'

Nat smiled. She shifted round so she was lying in Rob's lap again. 'I'd like that,' she murmured, feeling Rob's interest.

'We're doing nothing heavy this week, you're mostly resting and recovering your strength.'

'I was asleep for three weeks.'

His fingers touched her nipples. 'So we build you up slowly.'

She murmured in pleasure, stretching out, blinking, a little surprised to realise it was still raining.

Rob continued gently tweaking and caressing her. 'Do you feel like a little bit more stimulation?'

'Mm.'

'Good,' Rob murmured. 'Then how about you slide your hand inside your knickers?'

Nat blushed. 'Anyone might —' she answered automatically.

Rob chuckled. 'If it's too much for you. If you're not feeling horny –'

'It's not too much,' she whispered. 'I,' she wriggled. 'I like just being held by you, while it rains.'

Thursday 12th May

Douglas wrapped her in his arms and held her tight. 'Natalayiana. My dear almost-daughter. How are you feeling?'

Nat smiled, taking the seat offered. They were sat in the library and the room smelled heavenly. Books. Manuscripts. Old text and leather chairs and fine whisky. 'I'm okay. I still tire easily,' she shook her head. *You can sleep in the box in the ocean –*

'What distracts you?'

She smiled. 'That dream.' She shook her head again. 'I don't know if it's a dream, I'm losing my mind, or what. It's a recurring – it's like it's always there.'

Douglas nodded. 'Would you like something to drink?'

'Water, please.'

He smiled; poured and handed her a fine crystalline glass with water. Poured himself a whisky and sat down. 'So in the dream, you saw a glass box within the depths of the ocean?'

Nat nodded. 'I think I saw. It was almost like I *was* the water. And I kind of get – not quite flashbacks. But I don't know if I'm supposed to be scared of what's in the glass, or I am what's in the glass.'

Douglas smiled. 'Which do you think it is? Or are you scared of yourself?'

207

Nat nodded, tilting her head for a moment. 'I hadn't thought of that.' She sighed. 'I'm sorry, Douglas, I'm not good company.'

He chuckled. 'Nonsense. Let us talk of something different. You have not had a tour of Merryweather Hall, have you. Would you like that?'

She looked up and smiled. 'I would. Thank you. It's unusual, isn't it. The wings are single storey, but the central block isn't.'

Douglas nodded, standing up, leaving his glass on the table. 'Shall we start outside?' He offered her his arm.

Nat stood up, putting her hand on his arm. 'I would like that.'

He led the way outside, stopping first before the lake. It wasn't far into the woodlands and the driveway nor far behind them, but it was cooler, bracing, and pleasing to be surrounded by the tall, dark, trees.

'This was where I met the woman who would become my wife. Clovis' mother.' Douglas smiled. 'A very long time ago.'

'Not that long, surely.'

He smiled. 'You are too kind, Nat. I still remember being an uncouth youth, a spoiled rich brat, all those years ago. Thessalina made me mature.' He chuckled. 'She showed me an ankle. Nothing more. I knew I wanted more; we spent hours talking on the edge of the lake, she'd come for one of my father's interminable parties. She was as bored by it as I was.'

Nat smiled. 'Her ankle?'

He grinned. 'Certain things were not done in society. Or maybe they were, and my family were not a part of that society.' He patted her hand gently. 'Not getting what I wanted, for so long, helped me grow up.'

He took her away from the lake and deeper into the woodlands. 'I have always liked forests.' He sighed. 'This is not much of one, but it is private and deep. I came here, for days, when Thessalina passed. Screamed my rage to the trees.'

'I'm sorry.' She paused. 'You never thought –'

Douglas shook his head. 'She had my heart. Oh, I could have had affairs, I could have gone courting,' he shrugged. 'I am old fashioned. Please tell me if I'm boring you.'

Nat shook her head. 'You're not. Thank you for sharing, Douglas.' She smiled as he led took the path away from the drive and the entrance. 'We so rarely get to spend time with anyone.'

Douglas smiled. 'I am glad you are over calling me Lord Merryweather as well, Nat. Lord Merryweather,' he shook his head. 'It always makes me want to turn, half expecting to see my father storming towards me.'

'Did he not –'

He shook his head. 'I think we were both disappointed in each other. I deliberately set myself out to be as different from him as possible.' He grinned. 'For him, class, wealth, privilege, were all that mattered. Maintaining that and none of this progress.'

Nat nodded.

'What was your step mother like?'

Nat looked up at Douglas and smiled. 'Kelly – saved me. I had – issues – going through puberty. She told me it didn't matter, that she loved me regardless.'

Douglas smiled. 'That is good.'

'She was – everything a mother should be. I would rant and rage, get angry, helplessly angry,' she shook her head, 'and she would hold me. Let me cry and scream. When I'd calmed down we would cuddle in her bed, watch terrible TV and eat ice cream.'

It had taken her a long time – a *long* time – to trust Kelly enough to change for her. Her Were had trusted Kelly immediately. Had, according to Kelly – which she could believe – fallen asleep in her arms.

If I can't be a mother, she thought, and the chances are incredibly slim, then I will adopt. I want – a family. I want to do for someone what Kelly did for me.

--

'I would like us to go to the doctors.'

Rob raised an eyebrow but didn't speak.

'I want to know – for definite – what my chances of conceiving are.'

Rob swept her into his embrace, holding her tightly. 'I am very happy to do all I can to get you pregnant.' He smiled, tenuously. 'But you know the actual chances are – small. There's no recorded details of any female Were –'

'There's no officially recorded details of any Were, either.'

He nodded, kissing her head. 'I know. Male Weres can – inseminate – humans –'

She kissed him back. 'I don't want to talk of insemination, Rob.' She grinned. 'I want the practical.'

He grinned, pulling her dressing gown open. She shifted her hips. He hooked his fingers into her knickers and pulled them down.

'Mm. On the floor, Nat.'

Nat sat, flinching. 'The tiles are cold.' She lay down, spreading her legs obligingly.

'I'll have to warm you up then.' Rob knelt down, hands on her thighs, tucking into her.

Part 4

Friday 13th May

'Nat!' Marianne smiled warmly. 'You look – lovely. Stunning.'

Nat smiled weakly. 'Thank you. I'm only in for a few hours today, I still get tired easily –'

Marianne glanced at the closed office door, beckoning her behind the reception desk. 'No, I meant – these.'

Marianne spread a dozen sepia, black and white and full colour pictures across her desk.

Nat stared. They were *her* in the cell. Fully exposed. Naked. But they had been well done, she had to admit. She even looked good in them.

'Why didn't you tell me you were modelling?' Marianne whispered. 'I think it's very brave of you, Nat. Full nudes.' She smiled, matronly. 'And you do have a lovely bush and a lovely chest. I can see why Clovis Merryweather adores you.'

Nat blinked. 'Where did you get them?'

Marianne frowned. 'You sent them to me.'

Nat shook her head, fighting against the bottomless void threatening to open up beneath her. 'No, I didn't.' She closed her eyes. 'Homes for Weres kidnapped me from my house. Last year. They stripped me, put me in a cage, threatened to torture Rob and Gerald,' she shuddered.

Marianne frowned. 'But you look –'

Nat clenched her fists. Not again. Not again.

Marianne was there, hugging her tightly. 'Oh, my god, Nat. How terrible. I'm sorry.'

Nat clung to her, trying not to whimper.

'Nat,' said Bryan, coming into the reception. 'We need to talk.'

--

'They what?' she demanded.

Bryan scowled. 'Homes for Weres – want you to meet them. They came over – last month,' he grimaced. 'You were in a coma.'

'And they've sent nudes –'

Bryan nodded. 'They say they've sent them just to SHiP staff. They threaten to send them to the press. From experienced caseworker to nude model.'

'But I'm not –'

'If you say you're not, you're not. I don't know what they're trying to do, Nat. This is blackmail, pure and simple. You should take it to the Police.'

Nat shook her head, desperately. 'They took me from my bed. Stripped me. Put me in a cage.' She looked up at the ceiling, trying to blink the tears away. 'They shot Rob. Raped Lucie. I thought they were going to –'

'My god. Is Rob –'

'Rob's okay,' she felt lightheaded, trying to breathe.

'And Lucie? Who's Lucie?'

'His sister. She was a client of mine.'

Bryan nodded absently. 'I thought the name was vaguely familiar.' He frowned. 'What were they after?'

Nat sighed. 'They wanted me to admit that I'm a Were.'

Bryan stared. 'Pardon?'

Nat sniffed. 'They forced Rob into my cage. He is a Were. They forced him to change. I was scared I was going to be crushed. He was in pain –'

'Rob's a Were?'

Nat looked up. 'He works for the government. They know.'

Bryan stared at her. 'Wow.'

'I can't go to the Police,' Nat almost sobbed. 'Rob's people will investigate.' She sighed. 'All of Rob's colleagues have seen me naked.'

'This is not – the first time?'

Nat shook her head bitterly. 'They sent some pictures to George's wife. I don't know why they're doing it.'

Bryan fetched a brown envelope and passed it to her. 'You should have them.'

Nat took it absently. My boss has seen me naked. Marianne. Thomas, she scowled. George. Evie.

She burst into tears.

--

Nat picked up the full kettle and flung it at Rob. He batted it away easily. She picked up a knife and flung it; another and another, only half hearing Rob's winces. Tore the microwave out of the wall and flung it at him.

He tried to swat it away but she heard the impact, heard his cry.

'Fucking hell, Rob,' she screamed, pulling open the drawer and throwing cutlery at him. Grabbed a rolling pin. Hurled it without thinking. Picked up the last remaining knife –

Rob was suddenly there, pinning her hands tightly behind her back, holding her against him.

She spat and cursed and tried to knee him. Tried to shift the knife in her hands to get at him but he forced her hand open, dropping the knife.

He held her tightly, not speaking, clamping her wrists in his hands.

'Bastard,' she howled again, wriggling, trying to pull free, trying to knee him again, trying to hurt him, trying to make someone hurt, anyone hurt, make someone pay –

He held her tighter, crushing her to him.

'Bastard,' she sobbed, slumping in his arms.

He released her and caught her as she fell, cradling her.

'Nat. I love you.'

She stared at him, tears in her eyes. 'Don't,' she whimpered. 'I'm a useless bitch.'

'No, you're not.' He stroked her gently. 'My Were goddess.'

She looked up at Rob. A bruise was forming on his cheek. There was blood on his shirt and it was torn. 'Rob,' she almost wailed. 'Everything's —'

'Natalayiana,' he spoke softly, gently. 'I want to make love to you. I want to break precedent and get you pregnant. Can you imagine,' his hand slipped inside her shirt, resting against her belly, 'being pregnant. Being the first Were woman to carry a child.'

Nat looked up at him. 'Why do you love me, Rob? I've thrown knives at you. I threw our microwave at you. A kettle.'

He kissed her forehead. 'You're in shock, you're angry and you're feeling helpless. You needed to vent.'

'But I could have hurt you —'

'Yes, you could have.' He grimaced. 'And that is something you will have to live with. If it had been Robyn —'

Nat winced. 'I'm sorry.'

'Sorry isn't good enough, Nat.'

She looked up at him. 'What must I do?'

'You're going to the convention tomorrow.'

She shook her head. 'No. Not now. Not with all this,' she indicated the kitchen helplessly. 'Marianne thought I had become a model. Bryan returned his copies. Homes for Weres —'

Rob shook his head. 'Stop feeling sorry for yourself, Nat.'

She stared at him. 'They've got pictures of me —'

He nodded. 'And the department will track them down. Bryan's are still in the envelope they were sent in; that will help tracking them down.'

'But we know Homes –'

'You are going to the convention, Nat. You are not going to let Jezabel down.'

Nat stared, remembering. 'Yes. She can't – she wouldn't –'

'You are going to go to the convention, and you are going to have a good time.'

'You can't order me to –'

'Natalayiana!'

She froze.

'Nat. This can be sorted. Your friend Jezabel won't go to the convention without you.'

Nat scowled. Sighed. 'I know.' She looked up at him. 'I don't want all your colleagues to see. To know.'

Rob nodded slowly. 'I can – not – report it, but it is an attempt at blackmail. If we report it to the Police, *they* will ask. If we do nothing and then find out –'

'Can we – do anything? Bryan said something about a meeting? I don't want to look, is there anything else in the envelope?'

Rob fetched the envelope over and opened it.

'Miss Harewood will meet with representative of Homes for Weres. Or these will go to the press,' Rob read. 'It's signed, H.Q., H4W.'

Nat shuddered.

Rob put the note back into the envelope. 'What am I going to do with you, Nat?'

She looked up at him, fearful. 'What do you mean?'

He chuckled, kissing her head. 'Life is scary, Nat. I've been – out – as a Were – to the department, anyway – for a while. People know. Nothing has happened.'

'But the press –' Nat protested.

Rob shook his head. 'If they published them, sent them to any media outlet – well,' he grinned. 'Firstly, they would give away any blackmail potential they had. Secondly, the feed from the cell is still part of an open investigation, even if nothing's being done at the moment. They publish, the department comes down on them once more.'

'But I'm –'

He shook his head. 'Homes for Weres are a big company, in the States, anyway. They wouldn't want to jeopardise that over here. You could sue them, the dept, the Police, they would all be bringing trouble to their front door. They would not want that.'

Nat stared. 'But I'm still naked –' she wailed.

Rob nodded. 'Yes. And you look terrified and stunning at the same time. But if we meet them – and I do mean *we*, Nat – then that is better. Someone at H4W still has – or had – access to the feed. I want to see them face to face. Find out what they *actually* want. Then we can deal with it.'

Nat nodded slowly. 'I've been stupid, haven't I?'

Rob wrapped his arms around her. 'No, Nat, you haven't. You were scared out of your wits, and now your worst nightmare has returned. But we will face it – together.'

Saturday 14th May

Nat dressed quickly in red stockings and suspender belt; black knickers. A red slip and then a black blouse, fully buttoned –

'No,' Rob said, coming into the room behind her, his hands trailing over her rump, 'unbutton it a bit. Let people see a flash of red.'

Nat blushed a little, glancing at him. 'You wouldn't mind?'

Rob snorted, holding her, rubbing his hips against hers. 'If there was time, I would take your knickers down now and take you.' He chuckled. 'You will have to put the costume on again tomorrow when you get in.' He caressed her belly. 'My Were goddess in masquerade.'

Nat smiled shyly. She reached for the black skirt.

'You could do without the skirt.' Rob drew the material of her knickers between her cheeks, cupping and squeezing them. 'I would like to see you walking round in public in just that.'

Nat blushed. 'My fur spills out all over the place. And I'm not going – to expose myself. I'm there to support Jezabel.'

Rob grinned, kneeling behind her, giving her cheeks a nip. 'Put your skirt on then. We'll have some fun tomorrow evening.'

Nat reached for the skirt again. Rob slipped his hand between her thighs, resting his fingers on her.

'You are beautiful, Nat. You don't deserve all the shit you've been getting, but you – *we* – will get through this.' He stroked her gently. 'And I will do all I can tomorrow night to make you forget everything unpleasant.'

Nat murmured. It was lovely being gently stroked *there*.

He kissed her bottom. 'We should be going. Jezabel will be waiting.'

--

Nat stared. Felt like running. Jezabel grasped her hand tight.

Cool jazz music was playing. There was an upright piano in one corner; someone was actually sat at it, playing the music. There were clusters of traders' stalls with break out areas between. People dressed up as animals – or as humans, but with tails, whiskers and skimpy costumes. A solid background of muted conversations. She saw several couples kissing or feeling each other up.

'Was there anything – particularly –' she asked Jezabel, waving the programme she had in her hand.

Jezabel took the programme off her. She'd washed the costume and fluffed it; with the wig with squirrel ears, she really did look – bizarre. Like a human sized squirrel wearing a thong. But by no means was it the worst costume, at all.

A space cleared in the crowd and she saw for an instant a straw-gold haired, thin, woman. The woman had a completely feline made-up face, with whiskers, tufted ears and a cat-nose; was wearing pasties, a thong, stockings and a cat tail that she waggled and twitched.

'Wow,' breathed Jezabel, 'that's some costume.'

Nat nodded. 'There are some serious – *furries* – here.'

Jezabel nodded. 'You look lovely in your masquerade costume, Nat. If – I get any – will you make yourself scarce for a while?'

She nodded. 'Of course. Was there anything – particular – you wanted to see, or shall we just start looking at the traders' stalls?'

Jezabel shook her head. 'Everything,' she breathed.

--

'My god, that's a nice squirrel costume,' said the fifth person who'd stopped her, nodding towards Jezabel.

Four or five people surrounded Jezabel, hands openly stroking or touching her hips, thighs, buttocks. She was doing well, openly accepting the caresses, though Nat had seen her smack one hand away from getting too personal.

'A large chest, anyway.'

The speaker nodded. 'But does she capture the essence of the squirrel, do you think?'

Nat blinked, looking at the speaker. 'Sorry. What?'

'The essence of,' the man, blond haired and dressed like a normal, albeit for a pair of rabbit ears, said.

'Oh, this is furry but this is not *just* furry.' He grinned. 'Your first furry convention?'

Nat nodded, feeling – swamped.

'Take me,' the man said, 'by the way, the name's Rupert.'

Nat smiled blandly.

'Anyway,' he continued, 'I've more in common with a rabbit than the majority of people here. I'm not a furry.' He shuddered. 'But *Furry by Convention* isn't just about furries. It's about those who have a spirit guide. Or were born with the soul of an animal.'

'Your – animal's – a rabbit?' Nat asked.

He – Nat had already forgotten his name – shook his head. 'I have a reborn rabbit soul. Five exes and seven children.' He sniggered.

Nat shook her head. 'Nice to meet you.'

--

'How is it, Jezabel?'

Jezabel grinned, hugging her quickly. 'It's brilliant,' she whispered, smiling. 'Thank you, Nat.' She hugged Nat again, whispering in her ear, 'someone's given me their room number. Told me to come round later.'

Nat nodded. 'Be careful. But enjoy it.'

Jezabel grinned. 'It's the costume.' She waggled her tail. 'Lucky squirrel.'

--

'Who here has a spirit guide?'

Nat looked around. Several of the attendees in the session had raised hands. There seemed to be less –

dressing up. Not that they looked like – potential co-workers – either. More like hippies, she wondered.

'And what spirit creature guides do we have?'

Several creatures were called out. The host was a middle-aged man, thinning blond hair, running to slight podginess. He was dressed casually, but Nat could see the ends of tattoos on his wrists.

Jezabel wanted one, she remembered.

'Okay. What does your spirit guide give you?'

--

Nat flopped down into the seat in the restaurant. The lights were dimmed and there was hardly anyone else in, for all it was mid-afternoon. The waiter brought over her salad and lemon drink and she smiled in gratitude.

'Your first convention?'

Nat nodded. 'Yes.'

He grinned. 'It can get overwhelming for newcomers. Are you staying here for the weekend?'

She nodded again.

'The top three floors,' he grinned. 'Anything goes.' He made his way back to the counter.

Nat ate her salad in peace. Jezabel seems to be enjoying herself. She sighed. What am I to do about the photos? Did I overact? If Rob had been hurt, if he'd left –

'May I join you?'

Nat looked up, surprised. A tall, black haired, woman stood beside the table, a plate of food in her hands. She glanced at the other tables. 'Of course.'

The woman sat. Smiled at her. 'Thank you. I often find, in conventions like these, being sat on your own is enough for some people to proposition you.'

Nat smiled politely, taking a drink of her lemonade.

'My name is Emma, by the way.' The woman smiled. 'I'm a trader here. I'm not trying to seduce you.'

Nat blushed. 'I didn't –' she squirmed a little. 'My name's Nat. Natalayiana.'

Emma nodded. 'Your first convention?'

She nodded. 'Yes. I came here to support a friend. She's enjoying herself.'

'And you?' Emma asked, tucking into her food.

'I was,' Nat blushed, 'I was hoping to bump into a friend. Daiandrea. She's the –'

'The organiser,' Emma smiled. 'She's in her room at the moment. I can give you the number?'

Nat stared. Felt a little bad. 'Yes, please.'

--

'Daiandrea,' she stared speechlessly.

Daiandrea was combing her hair. She was wearing a silk dressing gown, open. Beneath it she was wearing what looked like leather underwear, encrusted with hundreds of tiny mirrors.

She drooled. She'd been imagining Daiandrea ever since meeting her at Lord Merryweather's a while ago. Dreamed – fantasied about having Daiandrea play with her –

'Can I help you?' Daiandrea asked, closing her gown.

Nat pushed the mask up. 'Sorry. Nat. We met – you gave me –'

'Natalayiana,' Daiandrea smiled, releasing her gown, letting it fall open again. 'Come in, Samantha's not long gone back out there.'

'Is it going well?'

Daiandrea took her by the hands and looked her up and down. 'Red and black, Nat. A classic look.'

Nat blushed. She blushed even more when Daiandrea undid a couple more of the buttons of her blouse.

'Show off the red, Nat. Don't be scared.' Daiandrea smiled.

'What are you,' Nat felt hot; felt her tongue was too big for her mouth. 'Are you – dressing as something?'

Daiandrea chuckled. 'I am dressing as Daiandrea, a one of a kind woman.' She studied Nat. 'You seem quite – enraptured – with the mirrored bra and knickers.'

Nat blushed furiously, shaking her head. 'No, no, I'm not. I mean,' she wiped her brow, 'I've never seen – underwear like it.'

Daiandrea laughed. It was a beautiful sound. A sound to wrap yourself in. A sound to dance naked in. A sound she wanted to hear more of.

--

Nat opened the door, wondering if the card wasn't working, the door seemed to be unlocked –

She paused in the doorway, staring.

Jezabel was on their bed, kissing a man whose hands were all over her chest. Another man knelt behind her, thrusting into her.

Nat withdrew.

--

'Nat?' She was shaken awake.

Daiandrea was sitting beside her. She was in the restaurant, now in darkness.

'You can't stay here, Nat.'

Nat nodded. 'My room. My friend's – entertaining.'

Daiandrea shook her head. 'You can't stay here, Nat. Reception called me. There's always a few people – dislodged by activities, this weekend.'

'Can I – could I stay in your room? I wouldn't be any trouble.'

Daiandrea shook her head. 'No. At the moment Miss Kitty is up there in only a thong and pasties.'

'She was walking around the convention in those.'

Daiandrea nodded. 'And I'm the only one who gets to take them off her and ride her.'

Nat scowled. 'But she's,' she looked away. 'You can do better than her, Daiandrea.'

Daiandrea raised an eyebrow.

'Me. I'm interested in you. I keep seeing myself, naked, on the floor. You're rubbing my belly with your foot.'

Daiandrea shook her head firmly. 'For that sort of thing to happen, Natalayiana, you would have to be some sort of dog.'

Nat stared, her heart lurching.

'No other beast would I let curl around my feet. A cat might display her belly to me, Nat, but you are neither cat nor dog.' Daiandrea crossed her arms over her chest.

'Please –'

'I see you more – as something not quite domesticated. A wild creature.'

'Is there – anywhere – my – a friend brought me.'

A look crossed Daiandrea's face. 'There *may* be. You are naturally shy, are you not?'

Nat nodded. 'Yes. If it wasn't for Jezabel, I wouldn't have come.'

Daiandrea nodded. 'Do you put yourself on my mercy?'

Nat frowned. Shrugged. Nodded. 'If there's somewhere to sleep,' she sighed. 'I'm sorry, I'm making a mess of everything at the moment. I've got a boyfriend, I'm very happy with him –'

Daiandrea raised an eyebrow. 'So you want me to throw over my lady-friend to have sex with you, when you've got a boyfriend that you're happy with?'

Nat shook her head. 'This,' she sighed. 'This worked, in my head. It was so much better.'

Daiandrea smiled. 'Call it a favour. I will – personally – find you a room. But you will owe me and I will call in my favour, sooner or later.' She chuckled. 'You may find the cost for this higher than you expected.'

'You will not – think less of me?'

She laughed. 'You come to something that makes you uncomfortable for the sake of a friend. They're successful and you leave them be. You come on to me – not seriously, it's not like you tried to kiss or grope me. But you have a boyfriend.'

'I will do – whatever you want.'

Daiandrea nodded. 'You will. But we'll talk of that another time. For now – come with me.'

Sunday 15th May

Nat eased the door open cautiously. Jezabel was sprawled on the bed, on her own. She yawned, tiptoeing through to the en suite to check: Jezabel's companions were long gone, by the look of it.

She eased the door shut and bolted it; ran a shower. Almost tore her clothes off and stood under it, shuddering.

The smells. The sounds. She almost convulsed, steadying herself against the wall.

Daiandrea had found her a room, a shared room. It had been horrific. There'd been underwear in the sink. Half dressed, unwashed, bodies, sprawled in the bed and the two chairs. Snores. Farts. Grunts. So much – humanity – she shuddered, feeling sick.

If I – *ever* – think about doing this again, remind me not to. Or to get my own room.

She flinched. Groaned. *And* I made a move on Daiandrea. Not much of one, though. At least – she shook her head. I love Rob. I really do.

She shuddered. It. Stunk. She grabbed the soap and began scrubbing at herself. So much stink.

--

'So how was it? You've been quiet since we dropped Jezabel off.'

Nat glanced at Rob. 'It was okay.' She shuddered. 'No, it wasn't, actually.'

'Oh? Problem with Jezabel?'

She shook her head. 'No. She got lucky. Was in the room. I had to find – another.' She grimaced. 'I've showered, but I can still smell it. Hear it.'

'Was it –'

'A shared room. I'd,' she shivered again. Stroked the mask in her hand. 'I would like to do something in this,' she looked shyly at Rob, who was concentrating on driving. 'But I want a long cold shower when I get in, first.'

Rob nodded. 'I was surprised to see you in the same clothes. I wondered whether you'd not had the opportunity to change.'

She shook her head. 'No, nothing happened. There were – panels, and talks and things, but it was,' she shrugged. 'I don't think – I can see what Daiandrea is trying to do,' she couldn't help but shiver at Daiandrea's name.

'Bringing Weres into furry-space? I'm not sure from either point of view.'

Nat shook her head. 'No, she's trying to – I don't know. Widen conversations? There were people there who thought they had the soul of creatures, some had animal spirit guides,' she shrugged. 'Most, I would guess, were furries.' She tried not to shudder. 'There was an awful lot of skin on display.'

Rob drove into their driveway. 'So you don't fancy going in costume next year? Something to hide your face – fully – so you can be anonymous –'

Nat shuddered. 'No.' She stroked his arm. 'Give me time. If we find a deep, dark, woods somewhere, I'm sure I'll do something,' she tried to grin coquettishly, but felt tired. 'I'm sure you will be able to cane me and have your way with me, but don't make me go into an enclosed space like that again.'

'The hotel was that bad?' Rob asked, getting out.

Nat got out, shaking her head. 'No.' She grimaced. 'There were just – too many people. Pheromones. Humans in heat,' she shuddered.

Rob fetched her case out of the boot. Came round and wrapped her in his embrace. He smelled lovely, all undergrowth and homely dust. She clung to him, snuffling into his shoulder. He slipped his hand under her skirt and stroked her bottom.

'Shall we get you inside and into a cold shower?'

Nat nodded. He pinched her and she yelped in surprise.

'Come on, Nat. Let's get you inside.'

Monday 16th May

She lapped against the glass. She was the water and the not-water. The glass contained her, held her imprisoned. The depth of the ocean would not crush her. She was liquid. Loosed, she could do nothing but rise to the surface —

Nat blinked, shifting in the bed. She could feel her stockings round her knees; the bed was damp beneath her. She'd showered – a wonderfully icy shower that had succeeded in sluicing most of the scents and memories off her skin – and then Rob had brought her through to the bedroom.

Rob – had been quite thorough. It hadn't been romantic or particularly tender – he'd put her onto her hands and knees, admiring her thighs – through the stockings – and her cheeks, before sliding into her and having his way with her.

Not quite perfunctory – she glanced over at him, little more than an outline in the dark. The clock blinked 2:22 at her. I love him. I do. Why did I make a move on Daiandrea? Why such a – she frowned to herself. It was barely a move. Everything's going too fast.

She rolled onto her side. Tonight we'll do it properly. I'll get him to sit on the sofa. I'll kneel before him – it's different from what I did for Clovis. I can do this. That. You know. She blushed. I can kneel before him. Unzip him. Take him into my mouth.

Nat smiled. Tried not to shudder. I should plan a weekend away. Just him and I. Somewhere – with a private garden. Somewhere – she blushed. Somewhere we can fuck outside.

She reached out to stroke him but pulled back. Let him sleep.

She slipped her hand between her thighs. I need to go to work in a few hours. I've got to deal with those photos at SHiP. Homes for Weres. Maybe Jack will know who to contact.

She stroked herself gently. Daiandrea did look lovely. I wonder what she will make me do. She grinned. I should have felt her up but I'm glad I didn't, at the same time. She doesn't hate me but now she knows I fancy her.

Nat sighed. Daiandrea. Laetitia. Robyn. *Rob*.

--

'Please, sit.'

Nat took the proffered seat in the booth. She was in the Sweeney Todd pie shop in Castle Eaton, north of Oxford. Jack sat down next to her; he had collected her from SHiP.

'I heard you'd been – in a coma?'

Nat half nodded, looking around. She'd heard of Sweeney Todd's, but never visited before. They were in the basement, with exposed beams and tables and some chairs almost growing out of the wall. It was – slightly trippy and surreal, as well as being intimate and cosy. The pie shop was known nationally and internationally, and quite down to earth.

'This – is an odd place for a meeting.'

Jack nodded. 'It's the preferred meeting place for Homes for Weres.'

'They blackmailed me,' Nat spoke quietly. 'What do you know about that?'

He shook his head. 'I know,' he ran a finger around his shirt collar. 'I know this is not the way – I suggested. You will meet Hubert – Hubert Quadrille. He's the head man here. He's,' Jack shifted, a little uneasily. 'He's – a character.'

Nat scowled. She'd agreed with Bryan that she'd start building back up her hours. George was still off, thankfully. She'd seen Thomas pull out of the carpark as she'd arrived; he either hadn't seen her or wasn't acknowledging her in any way.

So now I get to meet my blackmailer. She sighed, silently. Rob was close by, she'd seen his car as they drove through the village. If it goes wrong – or I want more information from this Hubert – or Jack –

Jack looked up and she sensed someone.

'Am I not who you expected?

A man sat down, majestically spreading out his gothic rainbow tailcoat. He was slim, almost cadaverous; white face makeup, like a clown, and multicoloured long hair. His eyes were heavily made up; sparkly blue lipstick and a sparkly pink tip to his thin nose.

Nat stared.

'I am Quadrille. Hubert Quadrille, esquire.' He grinned. 'I have you speechless, Miss Harewood?'

237

Nat blinked. Shook her head. 'No. No, of course not.'

He chuckled. 'Frankly, my dear, this is a rather sordid affair. I am not comfortable with what has been done to you.' He reached into a pocket in his tailcoat and drew out something small, a leathery, violet, package.

'I have had all the footage deleted. My paymasters in the States are not pleased.' He chuckled, passing the violet case over to Nat. 'In there you will find two USBs. There are duplicates. The whole feed from the camera. All the images, the stills, that were created. They have been treated.' He shook his head. 'I have seen three of them. Lighting, background, that sort of thing has been tweaked, but they are still you. I do not wish to see you naked.'

Nat took the package blankly. 'Why? Why were photos sent to the office? To George's wife, Evie?'

Quadrille shook his elegantly coiffured head. 'I have been in charge only a couple of months. This island,' he grinned, his accent slightly European, 'I control the whole of it for Homes for Weres. My counterparts in the States control far smaller areas each, but they did not wish to break the United Kingdom up.'

Nat shook her head, slipping the packet into her handbag. 'I don't understand.'

Quadrille grinned. 'Homes for Weres – are all about the Weres. In the States, it is easy. They form packs. Over here.' He smiled. 'Over here, the Were community is – non-existent? Fragmented.'

'But why give the photos back? H4W were blackmailing me – trying to blackmail me into admitting I'm a Were.' She glanced at Jack. 'I'm not, by the way.'

The ringmaster grinned. 'It does not take the death of a clown, Miss Harewood,' he chuckled, 'this is me, by the way. This is not a performance.' He smiled broadly at Jack. 'Well, it is a performance in that every moment of our lives is a performance, we are different people for who we are with, who we are speaking to, who we are wishing to impress. Jack Frost here,' he jerked his head at Jack. 'Now Jack, Jack is a fox. I can see it in his brush. In his spine. His eyes. His jaw.' He turned to look at her. 'But you. Oh, Miss Harewood.' A black rose appeared in his hand. His eyes sparkled. 'Such tender prey. Caught by a gypsy curse, perhaps? Now what would you be, Miss Harewood?'

'I am not a Were,' Nat repeated.

'Of course you are not,' Hubert seemed to barely shift his fingers and the black rose simply disappeared. 'Cursed under a blood moon. What caused the first Weres, Miss Harewood? Why were they only identified around the time of the second world war?'

'I – do not know.'

'You studied – Shifter Studies – I believe, at university?'

Nat nodded. 'I did. It was – mostly guesswork.'

'But guesswork by educated people. What is sleep but death rehearsal?' he sat back in the bench, smiling as one of the assistants came over.

'What would you like to eat, me dears?'

'What are the specials?' Jack asked.

The woman, who must have been seventy if she was a day over fifty, rattled off a long list of pies.

'This is on me, of course,' said Hubert. 'You will join us for a meal, I hope, Miss Harewood. We are not – opposed.'

Nat raised an eyebrow. Nodded reluctantly. Chose a spicy chicken pie with no sides. Was reminded of Laetitia, and eating her food off the floor.

'Well now, whatever you are thinking about is certainly bringing colour to your cheeks.'

Nat looked up, blushing even more furiously. 'It was – none of your business.'

Quadrille inclined his head. 'You have a beautiful soul, Miss Harewood. I do not want Homes for Weres to be exposing any more of its carriage.'

Nat stared.

'I should imagine, when your colour fully returns, you will become the crimson queen.'

Nat blinked. 'I'm not – I don't – my hair –'

The ringmaster chuckled. 'Oh, Miss Harewood. You should be as proud as punch. You have held your own against Homes for Weres. They were so certain you were; that they had caught themselves one who could be a spokes-figure for Weres.' He settled back into the bench. 'The whole – Linksfield affair –' he shuddered. 'Homes for Weres will leave him to rot. He went far beyond our intentions. Created, I am sure, entirely the wrong impression of us in your mind.'

Nat frowned. 'Why – do you think I am so interested in Weres? I am a caseworker – I work for SHiP, I mean.'

Conversation paused as the waitress returned with their orders. Jack was having the spicy chicken as well; tore strips off it with his fingers and wolfed them down. Hubert watched him indulgently.

'Fear is a man's best friend. Or a Were's.' Quadrille took a bite of his meal; touched a purple handkerchief to his lips. 'Not a mouse. There's a streak of fire, of passion, in you, Miss Harewood. But why are you interested in Weres? Why do my employers think you are a Were?' He took another bite of his pie. 'These are exceedingly good pies, Miss Harewood. Do not let yours go cold. The innkeeper's dread is that is that the food is off, the beer is off, the clientele leave,' he smiled, wanly.

'I don't – you're talking in –' Nat began.

The ringmaster nodded to her. 'I can see it in your eyes. My mind races. Two black hearts are we, Miss Harewood. So many thoughts. A sideshow crime, a hall of mirrors. Homes for Weres want you to admit you're a Were and you do in the video, but it's obtained under duress. No Reverend or lawyer, no Police,' his mouth twitched, ever so slightly, 'would accept it. And it is not what we want.'

He pushed his plate away. Without her noticing, he'd eaten the whole pie.

'If it gets exposed that Homes for Weres attempted to blackmail you, Miss Harewood, what do you think would happen?'

'The Police. Certain – departments.'

Quadrille nodded. 'I am ringmaster of Homes for Weres over here. Weres – are a clockwork boy. They must keep winding themselves up. Down the rabbit hole, a thing possessed. To bring us to the public's attention for attempted blackmail to bring a Were out into the open,' he shook his head, slamming his palm down on the table.

Nat jumped in surprise.

'No, Miss Harewood. That is not the kind of hunting party I am leading.' He chuckled. 'Miss Harewood, you look – overwhelmed.'

She shook her head. Took a small piece of her pie. 'No. I'm – I've never been here before. What you're saying,' she frowned. 'You're a trickster. A coyote. A rogue. A pied piper, leading people with your words.'

Quadrille burst into laughter. 'Oh, Miss Harewood, you are so right.' The laughter dropped from his face instantly. 'There's something in the cellar. Submerged at the orphanage. Chains are snapping, the demon box is breaking –'

Nat stared.

'But of course,' Hubert continued, 'do not all leaders lead people with their words. I know words have power. I know the power of a good show.' He grinned. 'Welcome back my friends, to the show that – welcome to my nightmare. In the dead of night, in the dark faery woods, do you not see the ghost ship? Do you see the riders of apocalypse? Something is coming, Miss Harewood. Something –' he chuckled. 'Something deliciously malevolent. And I aim to know, at the least, who the pieces are, who the players are, when Armageddon breaks upon us.'

Nat shook her head. Jack steadfastly ignored the ringmaster, polishing off the potatoes and vegetables he'd ordered.

'This is – I have no idea what you are talking about.'

Hubert chuckled. 'The girl who raised the dead.' He sat back in the bench. 'You were dead inside, Miss Harewood. Dying. One grey hair at a time. An engagement to the final death.'

Nat shook her head. 'You knew about –' she looked away. Gerald was with you – at the cell. Of course they knew; they manipulated Lucie into –

'Changes are coming, Miss Harewood. Weres cannot remain hidden forever. And you,' he raised a glass to her, 'are you the mothman or the lizard lady? The haunting or the mesmerist, drawing everyone in so that no one actually sees.' He smiled. 'It was – genuinely – a pleasure to meet you. You are so much more than a pawn, though you do not know yourself, yet.' He chuckled. 'Homes for Weres are not a threat to you, Miss Harewood. We may even be an ally.' He knocked the glass of water back. 'Jekyll and Hyde. Or the banshee, bringing down the old houses, the old powers.' He stood up. 'I will pay the bill upstairs. Jack, escort our lady of the forest back to SHiP, when you are done.'

He inclined his head to her. 'We will meet again, Miss Harewood. Lady Nightshade. Broken and remade. I thank you for your time.'

--

'Hi, Jezabel.'

Jezabel grinned, hugging her tightly. 'Thank you.' She stepped back to give Nat room to get past. 'I didn't get a threesome when I was,' she shrugged.

Nat smiled. 'Was it everything – you hoped?'

Jezabel grinned. There were more pictures up on the walls and the kitchen door was open. A faint breeze wafted through.

'The costume was fantastic! Someone just wanted me to chirrup while we –' she sniggered. 'They couldn't stop talking about how much they loved the idea of fucking a squirrel! And I had another bloke in a corridor!' She smirked. 'We're definitely going next year, Nat!' She sniggered. 'And my god. I brought a couple back to the room. They took turns, one fucked me while I gave the other a blow job.'

'I'm pleased for you.'

'Did you get to fuck the woman you were after? I woke up during the night and you weren't there. Figured you'd got yourself some tail.'

Nat shook her head. 'No. I did get to talk with her. But I'm not –'

Jezabel grinned. 'No? But Rob,' she made a noise of enjoyment. 'I bet he satisfies you and goes *deep*.' She leered.

Nat blushed.

'Well?' Jezabel prompted. 'Is he as big as he looks he is?'

Nat blushed even brighter.

'Are you telling me, in that red and black harlequin look, with the mask, that he didn't take you home and fuck you senselessly?'

Nat nodded shyly. 'We did – fuck.'

Jezabel grinned. 'How long have you been going out with Rob now?'

'About – nine months.'

'Have you taught him how you like to be eaten yet?'

Nat blushed shyly. Nodded. 'It was,' she managed to smile, 'the first – thing – he did.'

Jezabel grinned. 'Good.' She sat down, gesturing to the sofa. 'Thank you, Nat. I mean it. I really appreciate it. But –'

'But?'

Her client cum would-be friend nodded. 'I wanted – I needed – to know. Even if it was just for five minutes. But,' she smiled broadly. 'I got myself well taken care of. Next year –'

Next year I'm not going or I'm getting a separate room.

'Next year, by next year, I'd like to,' she pulled her jumper down and bra aside, 'have these so that blokes want to kiss them. That means getting a tattoo, to cover all the times I've sliced them up.'

Nat nodded. Jezabel tucked herself back in.

'Will you come with me? Get a tattoo with me?'

'I'll definitely come with you.'

'Will you get a tattoo with me? Think how much fun it'll be, taking your top down and showing Rob your tattooed – tits.'

Nat went to shake her head but stopped herself. The tattoo won't stay. Once I change – it'll be a waste. But. She tried not to blush. The thought of being in a tattooist's chair – I have no idea what a tattoo studio is actually like. But for that, I'd have to be topless. Topless before at least one complete stranger.

She nodded slowly. 'I'll do it.'

--

'How was it?'

Nat shook her head as Rob came and sat next to her on the sofa.

'It was – unexpected.'

He grinned. 'Well, I guessed you didn't need me.'

Nat nodded, removing the leathery packet she'd been given. It did, indeed, contain two USBs, though she'd not checked them.

'His name is Hubert Quadrille. He was dressed as some sort of – ringmaster.'

'And those?'

'USBs. Apparently he's killed the feed, removed everything from their computers. Just those copies left.'

Rob raised an eyebrow.

Nat shrugged. 'He was – I don't know. But I think I trust him. He was,' she breathed out, shaking her head. 'A showman. But it wasn't all flash.'

Rob put his arm round her shoulders. She wriggled in against him. 'I liked Sweeney Todd's. We should go there.'

'They are a good pie shop.'

She nodded. 'He said his bosses in the States weren't pleased with him. But he runs H4W over here.'

Rob hummed.

'What do you know about H4W? Has your department found anything out?'

'No. There was a shakeup after Linksfield. He could have come in then. No one has attempted to visit Linksfield in prison. No one has attempted to return to their site.'

'You're not – convinced?'

Rob shook his head. 'I didn't get to meet him. It was still – an attempt at blackmail, even if only to come to the meeting.'

'Jack did say he was a character.'

Rob hummed again. Nat took his hand, drew her shirt up and laid his hand against her belly.

'I need – skin on skin contact.'

'I'm not objecting,' he chuckled. 'How are you feeling?'

Nat wriggled up against him. Rob was warm and earthy, undergrowth-y and dusty smelling. 'Like I want to sleep. Jezabel's already making plans for next year's *Furry by Nature.*'

Rob chuckled.

'George is not back yet, fortunately. Thomas I only saw in passing, thankfully.'

'What happened – with George?'

Nat shook her head. 'Nothing, really. He tried to come on to me. Tried to pin me against a desk, but he didn't grope me or anything.' You didn't – *even* – grope Daiandrea. You'll never roll on the floor at her feet and have her rub your belly with her foot.

'And what did Bryan do?'

'George tried to hand his notice in. Bryan gave him a month off. Anger management meetings and things. He's still madly in love with Evie,' she shrugged.

Rob snorted. 'So he can afford a new case worker, can give George a month off, but won't restore your pay.'

Nat shrugged. 'I don't know. I feel like.' She sighed. 'Like it's mattering less. But nothing's changed.'

Rob stroked her. 'Everything's changed, Nat. You've spent three weeks in a coma. You're – responsible – for Clovis; for controlling his access to a hooker, anyway. You've met the head of the company who were blackmailing you, who've caused – an awful lot of hassles. But for them –'

Nat nodded. 'If they'd not sent the photos to Evie –' she scowled. 'I – couldn't seem to think of any of that in the meeting. Hubert was so –' she shook her head. 'I don't know. I would like to meet him again. Maybe you can be there. I'll see if Jack will arrange it. See if I can find out more from him.'

'Just be careful. There's still a lot about Homes for Weres that we don't know.'

Nat nodded. 'I will. Jezabel wants to get a tattoo.'

Rob didn't answer.

'She wants me to go with her. To get one at the same time as her.'

'When you shift –'

Nat nodded. 'I know. It'll blur, I'll lose it.' She paused. 'But I am tempted. Jezabel's getting a tattoo on her chest. She used to self-harm, cut herself, quite a bit. She wants something – that incorporates it. Hides it.'

She felt Rob shrug. With his free hand he stroked her arm.

'If I got one, on my chest, I would have to sit – topless – in front of a complete stranger.'

'And you like that idea?'

She could feel the warmth in his voice, the interest from his body.

'I'd have to meet them first. But yes, one complete stranger, I think so. As long as I think they're – okay, before the session.'

'We would have to get – loads – of photos of you topless with it, before you change.'

Nat blushed. 'Why?'

Rob chuckled. 'So that in fifty years, when we've hardly aged, we'll be able to look back and see where those blurred markings on your chest came from.'

'Do we – hardly age?'

Rob slipped his other hand inside her shirt. It was pleasing, a hand over her heart, a hand over her womb. My womb. *The water in the box*. My womb. She shivered.

'Cold?'

Nat shook her head. 'No, I was just,' she made a conscious decision not to mention the water or the glass box. 'I wouldn't object if you stopped just holding and started stroking.'

Rob bit her ear, tugging her head backwards as he pushed his hand inside her knickers.

Tuesday 17th May

'Why the secrecy?' Nat asked, sitting beside Uriah on the park bench. They were in the Cotley cemetery, one of the few green-ed areas in that part of Oxford.

Uriah chuckled. 'I am being,' he shrugged. 'Hopefully over cautious. But I would advise discretion as well, Miss Harewood.'

Nat frowned. 'I'm happy for you to call –'

'I have something to ask you. And,' he smiled, thoughtfully, 'once that matter is raised, something to tell you.'

Nat nodded. 'What do you want to ask?'

Uriah made a point of looking around carefully before answering. 'I know you are aware – of the Were situation.'

'The Were situation? Nat looked around cautiously. 'In what way?'

'In the Jack Mathers way.' He looked at her.

'Jack works for Home for Weres –' she blinked. 'He said – someone – found him a new place to live?'

Uriah nodded. 'There were three of us. We each had our own resources. We would hear of Weres who were afraid they'd been found out, who just needed to move, who wanted away from whatever situation they were in.'

Nat nodded.

'Weres would move around. We got a number of people out of – potentially bad situations. No one has

251

stepped up and said they are a Were. For,' he paused. 'No one is a nobody. But for someone without media attention, to be revealed as a Were.' He shook his head. 'There are those who believe in the miraculous powers of Were blood.' He looked away. 'And they are miraculous,' he muttered. 'There are several groups who would be interested in an unprotected Were.'

'An unprotected Were?' Nat frowned.

Uriah nodded, glancing around once more before continuing. 'Imagine if a grooming ring, or the like, got hold of a female Were. She would be trafficked around and used, used until she was broken.'

Nat shuddered.

'I am sorry for such – indiscretion, Nat. But there is more out there that would harm a Were than would support a Were. There were three of us who did what we could.'

'Three of you?'

Uriah nodded. 'Yes, Nat.' He smiled softly. 'Vic was one of them. He had a string of properties throughout Oxfordshire and further afield. Inconsequential, nothing special, two up, two down houses in poor, run-down areas. Places a Were could hide in the background, in the anonymity.'

She smiled at the thought of Vic as an unspoken hero, saving Weres without recompense or recognition. 'What do you want of me? I have no properties.'

Uriah chuckled. 'But you have SHiP. You may –'

'I'm only an admin assistant,' Nat protested. 'They don't trust me –'

Uriah stared. 'You misunderstand me, perhaps.'

'Oh?'

Uriah nodded. 'Would you have said Vic looked like a threat? Like someone who may be doing something – radical. Dangerous.'

Nat shook her head. 'No. He was a sweet old man.'

Uriah sighed. 'He was indeed. Until a year ago or so, he would visit our – guests. Anyone watching would think a harmless grandfather, or some kind of religious nut, trying to convert the youth.'

Nat nodded slowly. 'And you think, if I visited people, Weres, potential Weres –'

Uriah nodded. 'If anyone was watching, and often I doubt there is, but being foolish is a sure way of screwing up, then yes. If you visited someone, they would presume benefits or some sort of social support.'

Nat shivered. Uriah and Vic. Douglas is probably the third. If it was them who got Jack out – I wonder if they have contacts with Homes for Weres.

Uriah patted her hand. 'I do not mean to be – rude – Nat. But you seem – non-threatening. Chirpy. You could pass any watchers without arousing suspicion.'

'And you think there are people out there –'

She stopped at the look on Uriah's face. A mournful scowl. He shook his head when he realised she'd seen his look.

'Who was it?'

He shook his head. 'It was,' he sighed. 'We've been doing this a while. At the start, we weren't sure. I don't know if you remember, ten years ago or more. There were hoo-haas in the papers all the time. Shock journalism.'

Nat nodded slowly, grimly. 'I remember.' There'd been various 'outings' of people at university, none of whom, she was sure, had been Weres. But still it had been a – concerning – time.

'Someone came to us. Said they were a Were, that someone suspected. We delayed.' He sighed. 'I caused the delay. I was concerned it was a trap, that we, in turn, were being set up.'

Nat winced. 'And they –'

Uriah shook his head. 'When we finally agreed to go round – just myself and one other – they were gone. The house was ransacked. There was evidence of a fight. We reported it to the Police,' he shrugged.

He paused, glanced around the cemetery again. 'Obviously we couldn't mention Weres. They had no kin, had been abandoned as a teenager.' He shook his head. 'They disappeared. Someone came to us for help,' he looked at her, a little sadly. 'I am not selling myself well in this, but I do not want you thinking it is some glorious game, some fun little thing.'

'I –'

He held up his hand to stop her.

'Think about it. You do not need to tell me now. It is – it could be – risky. But we have to help those less fortunate than ourselves.'

Nat nodded. 'I can't not say no. Even if it wasn't – ', she mentally berated herself. 'Even if I'm not sort of continuing Vic's work,' she stumbled on.

'Thank you,' Uriah smiled. 'Your friends' housing situation is entirely free of this conversation, I will do what I can for them. Have you been able to speak to them about getting something written in advance of the wedding, about their being ejected when they get married?'

'Not yet.' Nat shook her head. 'I'm meeting Alice again tomorrow. I will ask her then.'

Uriah nodded. 'Thank you. The more we can get done in advance for them, the better.'

Nat nodded again.

'Are you,' Uriah hesitated. 'I have something to tell you, Miss Harewood, which may surprise you. Or shock you.'

Nat blinked. 'Okay. What is it?'

Uriah smiled. 'It is nothing terrible. Nothing embarrassing.' He patted her hand gently. 'Though it may give you cause for thought.'

Nat nodded. 'Go on.'

'Your step mother, Kelly,'

Nat nodded, fearful.

'You have an aunt. Kelly had a sister.'

--

'I thought you'd abandoned me!'

Nat hugged Robyn. Robyn enveloped her in her embrace.

'I was worried – you and Rob needed time without me.'

Nat shook her head. 'I was at a furry convention last weekend. This weekend.' She shook her head. 'It was –' she shuddered.

Robyn raised an eyebrow. 'Didn't take you for a furry, Nat. Didn't think you were *that* kinky.'

Nat shook her head. 'No. I went with – well. They were a client, but they're kind of not now and sort of a friend. I'm helping them.'

'Was it a good weekend?' Robyn closed the door behind them. Mildred was lying on the sofa, wiggling her arms and legs, alert and awake.

'They got some.'

'And you?' Robyn asked.

'I love Rob,' Nat protested.

Robyn opened her dressing gown. 'Tell me you don't want to bury your face in my boobs.'

Nat looked away. 'You know I do. But Dr Gold –'

'What's that bitch done now?' Robyn asked, picking up her daughter.

'She came round – when we were sunbathing. Before – the coma.'

Robyn shook her head. 'No, she didn't.'

Nat nodded. 'She did. She looked in the window.' She blushed. 'She saw us – I had my face in your cleavage.'

Robyn hooted with laughter. 'Naughty, Nat.' She pulled her shoulders back. 'I've still got two full breasts if you want to have a cuddle and a suckle.'

Nat blushed. 'She summoned me to her office. Her lab.'

Robyn grimaced. 'What did she do?'

'Would you – please –' Nat waved her hand at Robyn's chest.

'You want me to – cover myself up? I do have a daughter to feed.'

'You're my –' Nat blushed. 'Temptation.'

Robyn sniggered. 'Good. Don't get me wrong, Rob seems like an okay bloke. But the Devonshire pair will know your teeth and tongue again. And I've certainly not had my last lap at that delicious Harewood pussy.'

Nat blushed.

'What did she do?' Robyn asked again, making no effort to cover herself up.

'I had to strip,' Nat looked at Mildred, determined not to look at Robyn, knowing she would blush furiously. 'She put me over her desk. Caned me with a ruler until I could barely sit, my bottom was so bruised.'

Robyn snorted.

'What's funny?' Nat stared at her.

'Now that, I would like to see.' She grinned. 'Or cause.'

Nat blushed. 'Rob and I – I think we will, at some point, ask you to join us again.'

'Good.' Robyn leered. 'It was *most* enjoyable being fucked by your Rob. He is rather a big boy.'

'Rob and I – we need to talk more. And I'm having weird dreams, after the coma. When things – stabilise a bit. It was nice – sharing you with Rob. Fucking you and knowing he was watching, he was enjoying it.'

Robyn chuckled. 'There are *lots* of things I want to do with you and Rob. As long as we're okay.'

--

'Where are we going?'

Rob chuckled. 'It's a nice evening. We're having a picnic in Sunnymead Park.'

'I don't know it.'

Rob nodded. 'Families often visit. I'm hoping, being the evening, it'll be quiet.'

Nat raised an eyebrow.

'There is a reason I asked you to put a skirt on.' He grinned. 'You were about to say something.'

Nat nodded. 'I'm still,' she paused. 'There's a lot, but –'

They drove in to the carpark; there were a few other cars, but lots of space. Rob parked easily and turned the engine off. He undid his seatbelt.

'But what?'

Nat smiled, still not quite believing the news. 'I – I have an aunt!'

Rob widened his eyes. 'Kelly had a sister? You didn't know?'

Nat shook her head. 'Uriah wouldn't say anymore. He's investigating. They might want to – meet me.'

Rob got out and went round to her side; she unbuckled and climbed out.

'Oh, god, Nat, that would be fantastic.' Rob swept her up in his embrace, holding her tightly. 'If she's anything like Kelly as you've described her.'

Nat clung to him. 'I know. I've missed her.' She pulled back from him. 'Kelly would have liked you. She would have liked how you make me feel.'

'And how do I make you feel?' he grinned.

'Hot,' Nat breathed. 'Safe. Like I want to explore, and not just you.' She looked up at him. 'I do want to – I want to get comfortable with – taking you in my mouth. Giving you a blow job.'

He stroked her back. 'Only if you've comfortable with it, Nat. I eat you so often because I enjoy it and you taste delicious.'

Nat blushed furiously.

'There is nothing like it, Nat,' he whispered, kissing her nose, 'the scent of you, the taste of you, when you climax. Pushing my tongue through that forest of moist velvet between your thighs.'

Nat squirmed, blushing.

He grinned. 'Now, take your knickers off.'

Nat stared up at him. 'What?'

'There's a few other people wandering around the carpark, none too close. Take them off, put them in the footwell or on your seat.'

Nat blushed, looking around.

'You've got a skirt on, Nat. Though I will be lifting it and putting my hand on your cheek as we walk.'

'Someone might see,' she protested half-heartedly. It's safe. Rob's with you. It'll be nice, to feel a breeze. Rob does a lot for you. He's trying to make me comfortable with nudity.

Before she could think about it further, she reached up her skirt and hooked her fingers into them, pulled them down. Rob opened the door and she dumped them on her seat.

'There,' she grinned.

'Indeed,' Rob grinned, pushing her back against the car, kissing her passionately.

She held his head in her hands, thrusting her tongue into his mouth, exploring. Felt his hand pushing her shirt up. His fingers pinched her nipple: she almost yelped, but now his tongue was filling her mouth.

Nat surrendered to the kiss. She could smell him, feel him, taste him.

Felt his fingers stroke her bush. Felt a finger ease inside her and yelped.

Rob grinned. 'I've always wanted to finger you publicly, Nat.'

'Anyone could see,' she objected, automatically.

Rob nodded, pushing her shirt up further. 'And what will they see – what won't they?' He chuckled. 'Your right nipple is bared. They'll guess I've got a finger or two inside you – speaking of which –'

Nat wriggled as he pushed a second finger in, easing both deeper in to her.

'Is this more than you can handle?'

'I can take more than that, Adams,' she countered, smiling aggressively. 'Your cock's thicker and longer than that.'

He grinned, leaning in, kissing and biting her nipple until she protested –

'Anyone might see!'

Rob kissed her quickly. 'I could turn you round and put you against the car.'

He moved his thumb and Nat gasped.

'Your choice,' he grinned. 'I will bring you now, or I can turn you round and have that lovely, moist, velvet pussy, accommodate the whole of me. If I do that,' and he waggled his fingers –

Nat gasped: he increased the pressure on her clit and she panted furiously, oblivious to all but Rob.

'Orgasm into my hand, Miss Harewood, or be taken from behind, in a public carpark, while I've got a couple of fingers up that lovely arse of yours.'

Nat clutched at him, shuddering, more than half blind, sweat pouring off her as she tried not to purr and chirrup in delight.

She came, shuddering and thrusting, whimpering, chirruping softly.

'Are you alright?' said a voice.

Nat felt Rob let her shirt fall back into place and pulled his hand back.

'My friend was just having a panic attack.'

Nat managed to blink the sweat from her eyes and look round. A little old lady, with an older gentleman a couple of steps behind her, were at the opposite corner of the car. 'I'm okay, thank you.' She smiled shyly.

The woman nodded, stomping off. The man had a closed expression on his face, a twinkle in his eyes as he glanced at the pair of them before following the woman.

'They could of –' Nat shuddered.

Rob chuckled, hugging her one-armed. 'You came in a public carpark, Nat.' He lifted his free hand. It glistened with her pleasure. 'For politeness' sake, I think you should lick it clean.'

Wednesday 18th May

'Hello, back again?'

Nat smiled tightly at the sales assistant. 'My friend will be with me shortly.'

The older woman glanced around. 'I didn't want to say anything – but is she special needs?'

Nat raised her eyebrows. 'It was a lovely dress.'

'But very,' the woman shook her head. 'Did she realise the whole of her chest was on display?'

Nat nodded. 'It is a wedding dress. It was designed like that, to show off the bride's – assets.'

'But a girl like that,' the woman persisted.

'Like what?' Nat asked.

'You should have a word with her. It's not – seemly.'

'Natali.'

Nat turned: Alice was in the doorway of the shop; she hoped she'd not heard the exchange. Alice was wearing a frumpy cardigan and oversized, shapeless jeans.

'Alice,' she smiled, walking away from the assistant and gave Alice a quick hug. 'I wanted to apologise for last week. For making you upset. For saying I didn't really think the dress –'

Alice broke into a big beaming smile and hugged her back.

'We'd like to try the wedding dress again,' she smiled, coldly, at the assistant. 'You know which one. And we'd like some privacy.'

The woman tutted but went to fetch the dress.

Alice frowned. 'Why was she like that?'

'Because she is a very lonely and miserable creature,' Nat said firmly, 'whereas you have a fiancée and a wedding coming up and are a lovely person.'

Alice beamed brightly.

'I've put the dress on the rail in the back,' the assistant said, returning to the counter, 'I doubt anyone else will want to go up into the back area.'

Nat shook her head but escorted Alice into the raised back area of the shop. It was set back from the front and octagonal, lined with wedding dresses and ball gowns and little black dresses. There were several full length mirrors and separate curtained areas for trying clothes on.

'Alice,' Nat spoke softly, 'people will – be rude to you. About you. Because you're different.'

Alice looked up at her.

'You know. They are already.'

'At the shop. They think I don't hear them. They think I don't understand them. They comment on my arse, my chest, my expression.'

'Oh, Alice, I'm so sorry.'

Alice shook her head. 'It's not you. You've never been rude to me. About me. You were worried – I would get a cold in the dress.'

'I was worried the priest – the audience, your guests, I mean – would be able to see your nipples.'

Alice smiled. 'They're just for Howard.' She went over and drew the dress down that she liked from where the assistant had dumped it. 'He liked your house. So did I. Your boyfriend's very nice.'

'Thank you.'

She took the dress to one of the cubicles. Pulled her jumper off and dumped it on the chair. She was braless but had covered her nipples with several sticking plasters.

'Hurts my back,' she offered, 'and I knew I couldn't wear it with the dress.'

Alice's jeans followed and Nat helped her wriggle into the dress.

'Stand up as straight as you can; pull your chest back. Let me have a look at you.'

Alice did so. Nat smiled.

'Howard is going to love you in that dress. You might want to be sure you line up the sticking plasters, so they're not visible.'

Alice shook her head. 'I don't want Howard to find – sticking plasters there.'

Nat smiled. 'Howard is going to love putting his hands inside the bodice.'

Alice beamed. 'It's nice.' She sighed. 'But I can't afford it.'

'Do you love it?'

Alice nodded happily. 'I've never looked so nice. And it's like I'm a real woman, with bosoms and all.' She shook her head. 'But I don't even know where we're going to live –'

'First off,' Nat interrupted her, 'I'm going to buy the dress for you.'

Alice stared, shaking her head. 'No. You can't –'

Nat nodded. 'Yes. I can. Promise me you will wear it on your wedding day, and I will buy it for you here and now.'

Alice looked down at it. 'It's very – daring.'

'The lacy bodice looks lovely, Alice. It's your day, yours and Howard's. Why shouldn't you look lovely and sensational?'

'Howard will like it. I want Howard to like it.'

'That's settled then. I will buy it and you will wear it.'

'I owe you for it –'

Nat shook her head. 'Consider it my main wedding present to you and Howard.'

'It's so nice,' Alice stroked the lacy bodice. 'So nice.'

Thursday 19th May

'Do you like the picture better, Nat?'

Nat glanced at the picture. It was a photo of a tennis player, walking away from the camera, her skirt raised as she scratched herself.

'It's a well known image, Clovis. It's,' she forced herself not to be over-critical. 'Thank you for taking down the other picture. Your father has good taste in pictures. Perhaps you could discuss art with him, some time.'

Clovis scowled. 'He doesn't like me.'

Nat frowned. 'Why do you say that?'

Clovis sighed. 'He blames me for mother dying. What was it like being in a coma, Nat? Did you know you were unconscious?'

Nat shook her head. 'I dreamed, a little. I was mugged, I remember someone slamming my head into the pavement,' she shook her head.

'What did the Police say?'

'Not much. It was a rundown part of Oxford. They're pursuing enquiries,' she shrugged. She remembered, for an instant, the face of the much older man who'd been with the group of youths who'd attacked her. I should write down what I can remember. Report it to the Police. They gave me a reference number when I went in to give my statement.

'It must have been horrible.'

Nat nodded. 'I've had better days. Apparently I came round at the hospital, and then went into a coma.'

267

Clovis nodded absently. 'Do you like the office now?'

Nat glanced around the austere room. The walls were still grey, but the skirting boards were now white, the light switch was yellow.

'I didn't know what your favourite colours were. Or what colour you would like in here.'

'Thank you, Clovis.' Nat smiled. 'There is no rush on this, but possibly a soft green colour.' She shook her head. 'That doesn't mean you have to rush out and paint it. Find some samples. A range of colours. Let me choose which one.'

'But I could do it quicker –'

Nat nodded. 'I know. And I know you're eager to do this, Clovis, but if you just chose a colour and painted the walls that colour, what might happen?'

'It wouldn't be grey anymore.' He brightened. 'You'd like it brighter.'

Nat shrugged. 'I might prefer a different shade to the one you chose. I might like the colour you chose. But if you give me a choice, there would be little risk of having to repaint it.' She frowned. 'Do you need to repaint it yourself? You could get someone in to paint it.'

Clovis nodded. 'I have money. But pa says if I can do it myself, I should.'

Nat nodded. I'll be paying off Alice's dress for a while, but at least she's happy. And she'll look beautiful on her wedding day. Even if, she thought a little waspishly, she will be practically falling out of it. I will still get her a wedding present, anyway.

'That's a good idea, Clovis. Don't spend money if you can sort something yourself.'

He frowned. 'But what's the point of having money if we can't spend it?'

Nat shook her head. 'It's not that. If you can do something yourself, you know you can rely on yourself to fix it. If you always run to someone else to sort your problems —'

He nodded glumly.

'Do you object to me — being in charge of —'

Clovis shook his head. 'No. You're easier to talk to than pa. He's quite old fashioned. You're not.' He smiled, but it seemed more like a leer.

'He's only — sixty-ish —'

Clovis gave her an odd look. He looked away for a moment. 'I take it, since you don't like the room, that Felicita —'

Nat shook her head. 'I can see you're trying, Clovis. I'm happy for Felicita to visit you.'

--

'How are you feeling?' Marianne asked.

Nat nodded. 'Well, I had a meeting with Clovis today. The hospital wants me to go to the GP tomorrow for a check-up, make sure I'm okay.' She smiled at Bryan. 'Hopefully I should be back full- time next week.'

Bryan nodded. 'Good. Thank you. And thank you for working with Clovis. Lord Merryweather has been very supportive of SHiP.'

Nat half nodded. 'What's happening with George?'

'He's going through anger management courses. And marriage guidance courses. I have –' Bryan hesitated for an instant, 'I've extended his break. I want him in a more stable position before returning to the office.'

'What happened – with the photos?' asked Marianne. 'I thought you looked lovely.'

Nat blushed.

'Marianne,' Bryan glowered. 'Nat was –'

'Yes, I was naked.' Nat looked at Bryan. 'I had a meeting with Hubert Quadrille. He runs Homes for Weres over here.'

'And?' asked Marianne.

Nat shrugged. 'I've got a lot more questions to ask him. But he was not what I was expecting.'

'Is that a good or bad thing?' asked Bryan.

'I was expecting someone – corporate.' Nat hesitated. 'He was more of a showman, a ringmaster, than a corporate suit. But I still wouldn't like to end up on the wrong side of him.'

'And the blackmail attempt?' Bryan demanded.

Nat shook her head. 'He says he's pulled everything. Cut the feed. Gave me copies on memory sticks.' She shrugged. 'I would still like it investigated further to see if it has been –'

'That must be able to be done –' Marianne demanded.

Bryan frowned. 'If he says they've removed everything, you might need a court order to go in and investigate. They would want to see everything.'

Nat nodded. 'That's why – I sort of trust him, but I'd like to know he's not just a fall guy, not just someone sent to fob me off. He was quite theatrical.'

Bryan nodded. 'Well, that's, sort of something.'

Nat nodded. 'I'm going to see Dr Gold in a moment. She might be able to assist – getting SHiP out from the WLO contract.'

'Thank you.'

--

'And why, precisely, would I want that to happen?' Dr Gold raised an eyebrow.

Nat wiped her brow. It was unusually hot in the doctor's premises. Security had waved her through without the usual full examination, though she hadn't recognised the security guard.

'Because I would be grateful.'

Dr Gold smiled. 'Were Legal Opportunities have gained what could be a valuable resource in the Single, Homeless, integrated, Project. If it's falling apart, it can be asset-stripped. If staff aren't working to capacity, they can be dismissed, new staff hired.'

Nat shook her head. 'This is the – company – I work for. I could end up out of a job.'

Dr Gold shrugged. 'So? What is your employment status to me?'

Nat stared. 'You enjoyed – our trip to the Peak District.'

Laetitia chuckled. 'I enjoyed humiliating you, yes. I enjoyed fucking you, yes, knowing your boyfriend knew what I was doing to you. Have you told him just how much you enjoyed it?'

Nat looked away. 'Rob knows – I did what I had to.'

She laughed. 'You are a good little bell-ringer. But I've had what I want from you, Miss Harewood. Please go away.'

Nat stared. 'But. The other week – when you'd been round to Robyn's –'

Laetitia smiled. 'I did enjoy caning you so thoroughly you were badly bruised and it was painful to sit down. But whatever I want to do to you, I can do it on pain of hurting Robyn or Mildred.'

'You wouldn't hurt Mildred!'

Dr Gold raised an eyebrow. 'It's the offspring of a Were. It's less than human. Under law, I cannot be arrested – no one can – for the murder of a child of a Were. It's living, but only barely. There is no recognition of that fact.'

'Mildred's human! You must know she is. You've been doing tests on her!'

'If you are going to get angry, Miss Harewood, I will call security and have you roughed up.'

'You like humiliating me!' Nat protested, 'I'm offering you the chance to do anything to me, any time, anywhere.'

'So, for the sake of your precious little company, you would walk naked to work? You would strip in front of Bryan and offer yourself to him? Or should I send you round to Evie, George's wife. She might like to give you a good slap-around.'

Nat blanched. 'You like – hurting me.'

Dr Gold waved her hand, distractedly. 'You bore me, Miss Harewood. Were I a man, I might put you over my desk and take you from behind, but I'm not, and I fail to see what I would gain in any such – encounter.'

'Rob doesn't know – I'm offering myself.'

Dr Gold raised an eyebrow. 'So?'

'So it'll be our naughty little secret. Unless you want to humiliate me later by revealing it.'

Dr Gold shook her head. 'So what would I want to do with you? I can have you stripped naked at any time. I'm not particularly minded to fuck you –'

Nat thought she heard a distant, dull whump, as if of a heavy door closing, or something large falling over.

'Unless you were a Were. I would be interested in exploring an actual Were. If you were to bring Rob to me, I could – possibly – arrange something.'

Nat shook her head. 'I couldn't do that. Rob would suspect, anyway.' She smiled, tight-lipped. 'He knows you're – dodgy.'

Laetitia laughed. 'Dodgy? I'll tell you what's dodgy, Miss Harewood –'

There was a louder, nearer, thump. Dr Gold lifted the phone on her desk.

'Security? What's that noise?'

Nat could hear the buzzing: a dead line. She frowned. Got up.

'That's odd,' Dr Gold said. 'I've a generator on site in case the power goes down. The phones should be working –'

Nat opened the door. She'd never been into the central block, where the laboratories and other facilities were; a corridor ran round the whole complex, with the offices on the outer edge of the building.

'Clear out here.'

Dr Gold stood up, coming across to her. 'I want to know why security haven't answered,' she strode past Nat, heading towards the entrance.

Nat shrugged, following her. I tried, Bryan.

There was a further thump, a whump, and the wall on the right hand side disintegrated in an explosion of fire and glass.

Nat could smell petrol – saw, dimly, her vision bloodied, that Laetitia seemed to be flying sideways – and then she hit a solid wall, crumpling in on herself, feeling bones break, feeling organs rupture, feeling fire all around her –

First and Last and Always

A sampler

Due late 2022

'You're looking very summery, Nat.'

Nat smiled at Douglas' compliment. She was wearing a long cardigan and a long skirt; had left the voluntary group early and gone home, ostensibly to change before going to Douglas'. She'd taken a hot shower, taking the showerhead down and angling it – just so – until it had made her very happy and spent. The cardigan was a V cut, showing off her notional cleavage, though she was aware the slightest chill would bring a couple of points to the attention of anyone who looked at her.

Not just that, but beneath the skirt she wore no knickers or anything. It was pleasant; unexpectedly pleasant, to be completely underwear-free. To not have her fur restrained by cotton or silk or lace; to have a wild and untamed thicket loose beneath the skirt.

When Rob comes home, I'm going to make him lie on the sofa. I'll lie on top of him and give him a blowjob. She smiled at that thought. Then I'll draw the skirt up and let him do me doggy style, front or arse.

She sighed softly. To feel him in my arse again. To have his hands on my chest, clawing at my nipples as he thrusts into me. I would like that. I want – I really want – to be with Rob. And Robyn.

She smiled at Douglas. 'Sorry, I – my mind drifted for a moment.'

He grinned. 'Make no apologies, Nat. You were smiling, beautifully. It must have been a nice trip.'

Nat blushed.

Douglas laughed. 'I will not ask. Now then, I have two guests I would like you to meet. I am,' he hesitated, offering her his arm.

Nat put her hand on his arm. 'Go on.'

'I do not know what to make of these two. I know I likely said something similar about the lady who runs the – furry – festival, but this pair,' he smiled at her. 'I would like your opinion of them.'

He escorted her to the study. The pictures were – Nat wasn't quite sure what they style or theme or intention was, but they were all of different blocks of colour, impressionistic and abstract and deliberate.

There were two women waiting for them in the study. One had dark brown hair that became raven midway down its length, almost reaching her hips. Her face seemed a little smooth, almost reflective, a little shiny. It made guessing her age difficult; Nat couldn't tell if she was fourty, twenty or seventy. She was wearing an austere dark blue-black dress, plain, unbuttoned at the neck to reveal a religious collar of some sort.

The other was taller than the first, short hair, blonde-gold. Blue-silver eyes and a piercing stare; she was wearing what looked almost like a plain wedding dress, though with a suit jacket over the sheer blouse. There was something sharp about her, about her gaze, that Nat found disconcerting.

The dark-haired woman stared at her, eyes curiously alive in a dead-looking face. The blonde-haired woman almost smiled, her eyes narrowing a fraction.

'Miss Harewood. May I introduce you to Katya and Wythy. Ladies, Natalayiana is a care worker, supporting those who might have slipped through society's cracks.'

'Ladies, aye?' Wythy raised an eyebrow. There was a trace of a Celtic accent, harsh but faint.

'Wythy,' smiled the dark haired woman, Katya. 'My friend, because she was born poor, thinks that she cannot be a lady.'

Wythy scowled at her, but didn't speak.

'Perhaps you could explain to Natalayiana who you represent.'

Wythy's scowl thickened, but at a look from Katya she clamped her jaw shut.

'Wythy and I,' Katya smiled. 'Represent ourselves. Or perhaps, me. I am not without – money.'

Nat nodded, wondering where Douglas found them.

'I am also interested in Weres. Very interested.'

'Oh?' Nat asked, hoping she hadn't looked too surprised. 'In what respect?'

Katya smiled, but it was cold; harsh. 'Weres are – pawns. They need to be free. Those who try to control them, use them –'

Nat blinked in surprise. 'There are companies – trying to control them? There are actual Weres? I thought they were an urban legend.'

Wythy stared at her in possible hatred.

'Ah, no. They are indeed real. The things I have seen.' She shook her head, looking at Douglas. 'I do not know what you thought would be achieved by meeting someone so close-minded, Douglas, but it was good to see you again.'

Nat stared at the obvious recognition between the two of them.

Douglas smiled. 'Relax, Katya. Nat is aware of Weres.'

Katya looked at her, eyes narrowed. 'You were testing me?'

Nat shook her head, realising there was something going on that she had no idea about. 'No. I wanted your full pitch, not the one you give when you presume someone knows something or is on your side. Start your pitch, and I'll tell you where you can skip to.'

Katya pulled a face. 'My brother was a Were. I say was, because I watched him getting tortured and shot.'

Nat flinched. Katya's face was almost immobile, only her mouth moving and her eyes alive.

'They shot him in the face. Silver, like it would make a difference. Staked him like he was some cartoon horror monster, wreathed around with garlic.' She shook her head scornfully. 'I watched them crack his ribs open. He was alive.'

Nat felt sick.

'I watched them tear my brother's heart from his body because he was a Were.'

Nat grimaced.

'That was,' Douglas spoke softly. 'I saw some of the news, the reports, Nat. They were quickly hushed up.

Most of the information was locked away under official secrets.'

Nat frowned. 'Why official secrets? If it was murder, torture, a serial killer, even a group of people doing it –'

Katya snorted. 'I come from a *very* old family, Miss Harewood. I have – resources. I have money. I have contacts.'

'And?'

'Nat,' said Douglas, 'Katya's brother was murdered. For being a Were.' He looked meaningfully at her. 'If anything, Katya is underplaying the influence, the capabilities she has. And she could not scratch the surface.'

'Who – what?'

Katya shook her head. 'They were very careful. Professional. No names. My brother and I were taken from different locations. I was – put into a position where I could only watch. They put my brother on a slab. Chained him up. There was no blackmail, no attempts. They were always going to kill him.'

Nat looked at Douglas.

'This is – something terrible to hear, Natalayiana, on a Sunday afternoon. But I believe, you may be able to help Katya?'

'Help? How?'

Katya smiled, her cold, harsh smile. 'This was twenty years ago. Wythy,' she jerked her head at her companion, 'wasn't even a teenager. I have two things left in my life.'

Nat stared. What if what – Homes for Weres did – was not their first time?

'I find Weres. I get them to safer places.' Her eyes brightened, bordering on crazy. 'And I find companies and individuals who seek to benefit off Weres, one way or another. There are plenty. Snuff films. Bodyguards. Blood transfusions. Prestige.'

Her eyes glittered ferally, almost baring her teeth. In contrast Wythy, who was scowling at her, was almost languid.

Nat glanced at Douglas. 'There is that – company. I've met their – regional head? Managing director? I don't know what his title is. But he might be interested in a conversation.'

Katya snorted, shaking her head. 'I'm not, Miss Harewood. Any company using Weres deserves to be taken apart. I do not hold conversations with my targets.'

Nat stared. For all his showmanship, would Hubert – with all his resources – wait, I'm supporting Homes for Weres against someone who –

Someone who's waging a personal vendetta?

Don't mention Laetitia.

'He – they – are trying to help Weres.'

Even Douglas raised an eyebrow.

About Steven C. Davis

Steven C. Davis is the author of 'The Bookshop between the Worlds' pair of alternate-Earth novels, 'The Lore of the Sælvatici', part of a folk-horror retelling of the Robin Hood mythos, 'Less than Human', a non-paranormal paranormal romance series, and co-author, with S. J. Stewart, of 'The Heart's Cog' series of NSFW action-adventure novels.

They are the creative director of Tenebrous Texts, a dark and alternative-flavoured publishing house. Through Tenebrous Texts, Steven has published works from Stu Tovell, Jon Hartless, and the debut novel from C. H. Randle is due out imminently.

They are the organiser of the 'Raising Steam' festivals and the 'Raising Steam' downloads – all in aid of their chosen charity, New Futures Nepal, of whom they are a trustee. The 'Raising Steam' downloads are a global phenomenon, gathering Steampunk and alternative independent and unsigned musical artists from the UK and around the globe.

They are the host of the Gothic Alternative Steampunk and Progressive (GASP) radio show which goes out every Thursday at 8pm (UK time). GASP plays music without borders and is deliberately eclectic, playing the best in unsigned and independent regardless of genre.

Bibliography

"Voices on the Wind", The International Society of Poets, 1996, ISBN 1575531097. 'Fallen Stars', page 90.

"Cornix Sinistra", Tenebrous Texts, 2010, ISBN 9780856514707.

"Fantastically Horny", Far Horizons Press, 2015, ISBN 9780995464148. 'Cleopticus and Haerne' page 69.

"Steam Flashes", Tenebrous Texts, 2016, ISBN 9780956514714. 'A flower blossoms', page 51.

"Airships & Automata", Cogsmith Publishing, 2016, ISBN 9780995496903. 'Celestine', page 23.

"Within darkness & light", Nothing Books Publishing, 2017, ISBN 9781975631307. 'The Prisoner', page 186 and 'You stand in the dark', page 187.

"Tenebrosian Tales", Tenebrous Texts, 2020, ISBN 9780956514721.

"Cornix Sinistra", Tenebrous Texts [2020 edition], ISBN 9780956514769.

"Texts from the Shadows", Tenebrous Texts, 2021, ISBN 9781914246012.

"Less than Human", Tenebrous Texts, 2021, ISBN 9781914246036.

"Rise of the Sælvatici", Tenebrous Texts, April 2021. Kindle.

"Lore of the Sælvatici", Tenebrous Texts, 2021, ISBN 97809156514738.

"Texts from the Shadows #2", Tenebrous Texts, 2021, ISBN 9781914246128.

"Barrow witch (The Sælvatici)", Tenebrous Texts, October 2021. Kindle.

"Therianthrope", Tenebrous Texts, 2021, ISBN 9781914246029.

About Nicky Rowe

Nicky Rowe is the artist behind the main cover image, and an unrepentant 80s addict, as well as the main mover behind the synthwave project, Nightlights. Nicky has been drawing mischievous cat girls and other similar characters for over twenty years, and has more recently used that experience "wisely" to create Kiki, the time hopping Nightlights cat mascot who features on many of the covers.

It would be fair to say that Nicky is ever so slightly obsessed with synthesizers and synth music of many kinds, and may or may not have once been arrested for discussing DX7 FM synthesis patch programming in a built up area.

You can find Nightlights at Nightlightsuk.Bandcamp.com

GASP's Trading Card #10
Fear Incorporated

Bio: Fear Incorporated are a theatre macabre band formed in 2008 and write dark horror Gothic music. 8 studio albums, 3 EPs, 5 singles and 2 compilation albums have been released on CD and digital download on various record labels all which have been well received.
Link: fearincorporated.bandcamp.com
Raising Steam: Appears on 'Raising Steam IV'. Raisingsteam.bandcamp.com
Website: fearincorporated.jimdofree.com

Listen to the Gothic, Alternative, Steampunk and Progressive (**GASP**) Radio show every Thursday 8 – 11pm (UK time). Mixcloud.com/stevencdavis10/

Printed in Great Britain
by Amazon

79134812R00163